SPECIAL MESSAGE T

This book is published by

THE ULVERSCROFT FOUNDATION,

a registered charity in the U.K., No. 264873

The Foundation was established in 1974 to provide funds to help towards research, diagnosis and treatment of eye diseases. Below are a few examples of contributions made by THE ULVERSCROFT FOUNDATION:

★ A new Children's Assessment Unit
  at Moorfield's Hospital, London.

★ Twin operating theatres at the
  Western Ophthalmic Hospital, London.

★ The Frederick Thorpe Ulverscroft Chair of
  Ophthalmology at the University of Leicester.

★ Eye Laser equipment to various eye hospitals.

If you would like to help further the work of the Foundation by making a donation or leaving a legacy, every contribution, no matter how small, is received with gratitude. Please write for details to:

THE ULVERSCROFT FOUNDATION,
The Green, Bradgate Road, Anstey,
Leicestershire, LE7 7FU. England.
Telephone: (0533) 364325

Love is
a time of enchantment:
in it all days are fair and all fields
green. Youth is blest by it,
old age made benign: the eyes of love see
roses blooming in December,
and sunshine through rain. Verily
is the time of true-love
a time of enchantment—and
Oh! how eager is woman
to be bewitched!

DIGBY

The story of a man whose many adventures ensured him great notoriety in his time. He was, at various stages in his life, scientist, philosopher, pirate and poet. Welcomed at courts throughout Europe, he was the particular favourite of the Queen of France who wanted him to be her lover. But Kenelm Digby loved another: the beautiful Venetia was the mainspring of his life, and on her death he became and remained a widower.

PAMELA HILL

DIGBY

Complete and Unabridged

ULVERSCROFT
Leicester

First published in Great Britain in 1987 by
Robert Hale Ltd.,
London

First Large Print Edition
published December 1990
by arrangement with
Robert Hale Ltd.,
London

British Library CIP Data

Hill, Pamela, *1920–*
    Digby.—Large print ed.—
    Ulverscroft large print series: historical romance
    I. Title
    823'.914

    ISBN 0-7089-2331-3

Published by
F. A. Thorpe (Publishing) Ltd.
Anstey, Leicestershire
Set by Rowland Phototypesetting Ltd.
Bury St. Edmunds, Suffolk
Printed and bound in Great Britain by
T. J. Press (Padstow) Ltd., Padstow, Cornwall

1

IT was like him to arrive precipitately, with a roar, into the world at half-past five on a summer morning, with a three-quarter moon still showing in the nether sky. His young mother—he was her third child, two girls were in the nursery and this time she hoped for a son —had known for some months that he was very much alive, having kicked like a galliard beneath her petticoats daily. She lay back at last in her bed, thankful that the ordeal had been no worse; the child had struggled and fought to be born since the waters burst yesterday, and now had come of a sudden before the midwife had time to hold his head. He was certainly a boy. She herself had been able to note, as they took him away to cleanse him, that his hair was brown and curly, plastered over a big wide scalp, and his hands surprisingly small, with tapering fingers. They were burning a shovelful of lavender now, to take away the smell of blood and humours; it was not safe to let the outer air into a birth-chamber. How glad she was that she had borne a boy at last! He would be heir of Gothurst and her other places, all of which she shared with her husband, for they both had land and money. Everard would be waiting now impatiently to see her and his son. For this, the women came and made Mary Digby seemly again, combing and dressing her sweat-soaked hair and putting on a fresh cap trimmed with point lace, and a wide-pleated bedgown to cover her breasts, which were swollen and bound with linen to stop the milk. As to that, the baby yelled for the wet-nurse before the good woman was ready; most babies slept.

Everard Digby came in then half-shyly to see his son, having waited up all night and foregone his beloved hunting this morning, in case Mary needed him. His great handsome presence—he was six feet and broad with it, his bearded face open and with generous features—filled the room, and the thought came to Mary that were her son to grow to be such another, she herself would scarcely be noticed between the two of them. Everard glanced at the baby and then came straight to her; they loved one another and as usual he had almost gone through the agonies with her; they had married when she was fifteen and he nineteen, but that was three years ago.

"You are not hurt?" he asked her, and Mary smiled and shook her head.

"Only tired. Look at our great rascal. I declare that I do not know how ever I housed him."

He strode over again to the monster in the cradle, and this time smiled. Mary watched him adoringly. The baby had been a gift to her husband, no more; everything was for Everard.

"We must have Father Gerard christen him when he comes again," she heard him say, and the waiting-women averted their glances. He was too outspoken, the master; there was no guile in him. There would be trouble one day at Gothurst, such as other folk had had in the great houses where they hid priests. Things were not so bad as they had been in the old Queen's time, but nobody was sure of this new King from Scotland, though it was said he had promised to let folk do as

3

they would. It was best to keep silent about such things; you never knew.

"Kenelm," announced his father with satisfaction, looking down on the brown head already drying out to fluff. An ancestor of that name had fought for Henry VI at Towton, with his three brothers. In the next generation seven Digbys, having fought for the Tudor, were knighted on Bosworth Field. They had owned land hereabouts since the time of Edward the Confessor; Norman blood was newcome. Everard was proud, accordingly, that he had a fine son to carry on the name.

The baby waved his fists, already groping for the world. Everard proffered a finger; Kenelm seized it in a sure grip. "See that!" said the young father. "He hath all his wits before his eyes are open."

He came to his wife in the bed again, laughing, and took her hand. "Will he take after my grandsire, think you? If that is so we will never be at peace." That personage, another Everard Digby, had been famous for his spirited lecturing and arguing and loud disturbance, having even been deprived of his Fellowship at Oxford for disrespect, debt, loud hallooing and blowing a horn there while all men slept. Worst of all, he had got up one day in the pulpit of St. Mary's Chapel and preached Popery, although the Digby family were Protestant. But even for that the earlier Everard had suffered no harm, so winning were his ways with all men; the Fellowship was restored to him later on.

Mary Digby lay content, her hand in her husband's. She had loved him at first sight, she, Mary Mulsho of Gothurst, her father's heiress; so much of Everard, and all of it goodly! Her father had been careful of her; he had wanted her to marry a man already rich, because then her fortune would not be squandered. It was after the marriage, in Everard's brief absence, that Mary had welcomed two strangers to Gothurst, one of whom in particular was adept at card-games and riding out hawking. It took time and caution to discover that he was a Catholic priest, to reveal whose identity would have meant his death. Mary had already some notions of the Faith; so she was received and was delighted to learn that Everard had also been received some time since, but without saying so to her, lest he seem to force her. Now they both drew comfort from the Sacraments and from the priests' secret visits to say Mass. Father Gerard, the hawker, had become a close friend. Kenelm should be brought up, without doubt, as a Catholic, difficult as it was for Papists nowadays to do as they would with their children.

The summer lingered, and when it was fine Kenelm would be taken out to lie and kick his strong plump legs on a coverlet on the lawn with its surround of green clipped hedges, not too near the pond where lilies still bloomed pale. Gothurst was a fine property, two hundred acres of good Buckinghamshire earth, whose rents enabled other things to be done besides payment of the recusancy fines, which had ruined many families. But Everard and Mary between them were rich enough to afford it. Kenelm began to feel something of that glad security, also coming to early knowledge that there was a world beyond Gothurst; folk would come in in little groups, riding or walking, plainly dressed for the most part so that they did not attract attention, staying for a while, then vanishing quietly as they had come. There was one who came often; Father Gerard, unassuming in hodden clothes, holding Kenelm up in his arms and one day, in presence of them all, pouring water on the child's head in the sign of the cross. It was a hot August day and Kenelm chuckled and gurgled at the coolness of the water against his skin, but did not know what it was about or what the words meant. He was still avid for milk, tearing at the nurse's bodice before she had time to open it and give him her full, reliable breast; seizing and sucking at that as though it had been his mother's. But his mother herself he knew quite differently; small, quiet, authoritative, always obeyed; even his father seemed to obey her. Kenelm adored Everard from the beginning. He himself had begun to crawl, talk, stagger and play sooner than other children, and crowed with delight when he heard the nightly hunting-horn which meant his father would soon be home: then there were his father's arms, the smell of leather and horses and animal blood, and his father would talk to him, pick him up and dandle him, teach him words, play with him, ruffle his thick thatch of curly hair which already defied the comb. Poor Johnny, the second baby, who came in due course, was by contrast quiet, dutiful and obedient from the first. It was as if all his life would be lived in the shadow of splendid Kenelm Digby.

They had Kenelm's horoscope taken early, and it differed in few ways from that he would have read later for himself: the Sun in the twelfth house, sextile to Saturn; Mercury square to Saturn, which meant many great enterprises, not all of them fulfilled. The time of the moon meant a sensitive nature and unsettled humour, which last Everard and Mary could have seen for themselves; but the Crab had its claws raised, and above all that was dominant.

"He will be a philosopher," said Everard. Mary laughed. "And a huntsman," she murmured. "No doubt when he takes a wife she will see little of him, for he will forever be chasing the stag."

"Why, my life, do I stray from home

over much?" He was at once contrite; he had such a love of hunting and sport that it was true he spent most of his time at it. Maybe he should become more dutiful, not only to his wife but to his position; there was much he could do, accordingly, for other folk. He would give it some thought.

"It was a jest," said Mary. She kissed him, savouring the roughness of his cheek. "You know that if you are content, so am I; and what would I do with you under my feet all day?"

"There would be less gossip with the old dame from Enston. I do not like the woman."

"She means no harm; she is lonely."

"Maybe." He was preoccupied with the thought that had come to him of his own duty. King James had taken three months to travel down through England from the poorer, bleaker north; feasting and hunting, drinking his strong Greek wine, being entertained richly by the owners of great houses, at Worksop, Doncaster, Belvoir, who wanted to stand well in the new reign; in no apparent haste to reach his capital. This was the man who had survived a troubled and dangerous childhood in Scotland to succeed at last, after much doubt, to Elizabeth's throne. James had always placated the old Queen, allowing even the execution of his imprisoned mother without war. What manner of man he could be had been much prejudged, and many had ridden cautiously to Edinburgh in the twilight years of the last reign to extract promises, which James had given readily.

Everard Digby, as an officer of the Gentlemen Pensioners of the Royal Bodyguard, met his new King at Whitehall and was knighted by him. He was amazed, and somewhat revolted; the King stank like mice in damp straw. He never washed his hands because he was proud of their whiteness; he dribbled when he drank because his tongue was too big. He was reputed to be a scholar, which was as well because he could not walk on his weak legs unaided. In his face the dark, disillusioned, heavy-lidded eyes of Mary of Scotland looked out over a thin short beard. James's speech was almost unintelligible to English listeners, and he brought a large train of Scots with him. To his interest however most of all was hunchbacked Robert Cecil, who by secret ways had done much to ensure him the crown, and was rewarded now by being made a viscount. Cecil, to do him justice, wanted peace with Spain, and all his careful attention to affairs in England was directed to that, and to suppress idolatry and Romish superstition. To Catholics the new King broke all his previous promises, being overheard to say as soon as he had crossed the Border, "Na! Na! We ha'e nae need o' the Papists noo!"

"It is good to have you here, and I pray there may be no danger. I do not think any know of your coming to Gothurst save those I can trust."

"We may trust in God."

Father Henry Garnet, Superior of the Jesuits in England, his homely face weatherbeaten with much travel, had contrived to remain hidden for eighteen years, riding between one house and another among the faithful in London and the Midland counties. Many times they had hidden him, often in the cunning priest-holes devised by Brother Nicholas Owen, by most called Little John, who was with him now; a short, stocky, outwardly unremark-able man who had long since got himself a rupture with lifting heavy building-stones, and limped slightly because of it, but remained cheerful and silent. He had devised hiding-places up and down England beneath floors, behind chimney-stacks, between walls and storeys, through dower-chests. Some would never be discovered; a few had been.

Everard, in his own house, suddenly went to the door and opened it quickly. There was no one listening outside; he had had to be sure. They were in one of the smaller rooms of Gothurst, looking out over the avenue of broad oaks up which, if they came, enemies must ride. However the master of the house returned, satisfied. "We may have a good supper," he assured the priest. "My wife is busied with the maids in the kitchen, basting and baking." A pleasant smell of cooking indeed reached them.

"A meal will be welcome." Father Garnet, who had fasted since morning, smiled gently. His replies were always predictable and indeed wearied some who thought him tedious. However he was known everywhere as the Lamb because of his unvarying gentleness. He had come lately from the Vaux house of White Webbs, with Mistress Anne Vaux, who cared for him there as his housekeeper in secret, riding by him and Little John. The watchful eyes in Anne's worn face scanned the group anxiously, then the windows. Danger could come very suddenly, and because Father Garnet had contrived to remain hidden in England since the bells had pealed for the Queen of Scots' condemnation eighteen years ago, did not mean that any one day was safer than the rest. On arrest, priests were condemned to a traitor's death with all its horror; she thought more often of that than that her own house might be ransacked and she herself thrown in prison for harbouring them.

Everard spoke. "Now that my wife and I have been confessed to our relief and have heard Holy Mass with joy, there is a thing I would ask." He tapped a finger on the palm of the other hand. "As you well know, the King is less steadfast in his promises of toleration than had been hoped by all of us. It was one thing to give them while he angled for the throne in Scotland, but a different matter, evidently, now he is on it. Cecil guides his policies against us still, although now there is peace with Spain; and the King there—they say his treasury is empty—dared not aid us even in the terms of the peace treaty, so fearful is he of an alliance between England and France."

There was a silence. Everyone in the room had heard of Robert Cecil, ennobled now, and fear of him was behind everything, daily. The small crooked man, who had inherited his position of state from his dead father Lord Burghley, bore a malignant hatred towards English Catholics and had vowed to root them out; and did his best accordingly with juries, fines, imprisonment and even torture such as had been perpetrated under Elizabeth.

"I would fain write to Master Cecil, viscount or no," Everard put in. "I would tell him the truth, that it is to his interest and the King's that there should be peace and loyalty in the realm now that Spain is no longer our enemy. Surely it would do no harm to him and the King to let you and other priests come to these shores freely and go about your good work, and we Catholics worship openly instead of in hiding: and to send recruits gladly for the English regiment in Flanders."

"Do not put yourself in danger," said Father Garnet.

"I would secure a better life for my son than one of juries, twenty pounds each month in fines—they say Cranborne Crookback—he cannot help his body, but he can help his mind—will introduce that for each member of the family and its servants for half that my lord pays now, and many will be ruined by it—and they believe also that worse things are coming. We have had no open champion since the Earl of Arundel died in the Tower, having lain there eleven years for the Faith."

"It is sad that Mary of Scotland's son should hound those of his mother's religion," said the priest, and Anne Vaux broke in. "He could not have remembered her," she said. "They were parted when he was but a babe."

"But he knew well enough she was in England, in prison, and made small effort to have her set free, and no clamour at all at the manner of her death."

"Well, she is dead," said the priest, and crossed himself.

"But we are alive, and want to live free. May I show you something of what I would write?" Everard Digby drew a folded paper from his doublet. The Superior glanced at it.

If your Lordship and the State think it fit to deal severely with Catholics, within brief there will be massacres, rebellions, and desperate attempts against the King and State.

"It will maybe do you no good to write that," said Father Garnet. "They say the King fears swords. He also fears, despite denying it, excommunication such as was sent to the late Queen, for it will lessen his power abroad. If you were to offer to mediate in such a way with Rome, they might attend to you in a better fashion." He sighed. "The King has had to tread many crooked paths in order to save himself. Maybe now that he is secure, and has gained his ambition, there will be hope."

"It was better before the old Queen

died, at least," said Anne Vaux. "No doubt she had more on her mind then, poor soul, than levying fines and harrying innocent folk."

"Ay, and Cecil—I must remember he is Cranborne now—would be too greatly busied with Scots affairs to attend to us here so closely."

"I will write, then," said Everard. He did so that same night after their supper, phrasing what he had to say very carefully and showing it, again, to the priest for his final approval. It went off by the riders, but days and weeks passed and no reply came. All that it had done was to have Everard Digby's name noted on one of the carefully numbered scrolls of paper which lay till required shelved in Cranborne's office in his town house in the Strand, where the garden, ran like others, down to the river.

"And so you are too idle to come on pilgrimage with us. I do not think our cousins' marriage arrangements should keep you from it. There is some other thing."

Mary looked at her husband reproachfully, and he stopped playing with Kenelm's fingers and looked steadily at her. "St. Winefride's Well is a holy place," Mary said. "The saint cured Father Oldcorn of a growth on his tongue lately."

"I have another matter that I must wait for." Everard still hoped for a reply from Cranborne, even a non-committal one; he felt foolish and betrayed. He was aware of Mary's disappointment that he would not accompany her and Anne Vaux, Father Garnet, the lay-brother and their own Father Gerard who had christened Kenelm, to the holy well in Wales. The Superior needed a holiday, and this was less dangerous than trying to get abroad. There was enough freedom in the Welsh mountains to have set up a Catholic printing press in a cave and issued pamphlets over a matter of years, some time ago; but it was closed now and the machinery confiscated. Yet the nature of the country itself made protection easier. In the end Anne Vaux, calling herself Mistress Perkins and travelling as Father Garnet's sister, and her own sisters, and Father Gerard with his expertise of card-playing and hawking, which no one expected in a priest, and Little John himself, and some servants, rode by Mary, who had kissed her four children farewell and left Everard to his waiting. By then there was a party of about thirty strong riding towards the Welsh border, dressed as ordinary travellers; once over the border, and nearing the holy place, the women of the party were able to take off their shoes and walk barefoot in penance, so safe was it in the green valleys. They came to the well housed in its ancient building among the slopes of the mountains; and received the blessing and heard Mass, which could still be said here daily. Refreshed in spirit, they returned home in a leisurely way, visiting Ambrose Rookwood and his beautiful wife, and Daventry and Rushton, where the old squire was on the point of death and his son Thomas Tresham expectant of a fortune. It had been a welcome respite from tension and unease, the August sun shining clearly throughout with little rain. Father Garnet, feeling much rested, rode off to Erith with a promise to return. Little John accompanied him as always: neither man was of an appearance to be heeded much on the road.

As for Kenelm Digby, he was brown with playing daily in the sun. "He has grown hugely," said Mary. She was no longer so troubled about her husband as she had been: Everard seemed to have shed, for the time, at least, whatever had been preoccupying him when she left.

Kenelm had a wooden toy sword, which had been his father's at his age. He would run and hit with it, or try to stab with it; but it was harmless. One day he was playing with it when his father came in. Kenelm used a phrase some nurse had taught him. "Top off y'head," he said, brandishing the sword. "Top off y'head."

Everard took the sword gently from his son, pretending to sheath it. "Use your sword wisely, my lad," he said. "Maybe, if you do, the King's own sword will one day make you a knight." He was glad of the relief of the child's laughter; within himself he had been, for some reason, remembering the young Earl of Essex and his rebellion and execution in the Queen's last days. So handsome a man, left dead in his blood!

Kenelm reached for the sword. "Y' dead now," he said. "Lie down."

Everard pretended to be dead. For instants his closed eyelids let the long lashes lie on his cheeks, which seemed pale like a dead man's. Kenelm began to scream without knowing why. He put his own large hands, with their slim tapering fingers, into his mouth to stop himself, but by now his father had got up and was laughing and comforting him. He wasn't really dead; how could he, Kenelm, live without his father?

Mary Digby could not like the two gentlemen who had come to visit at Gothurst even though one was, evidently, Everard's colonel in the Gentlemen Pensioners and held the appointment by grace of his kinsman, the Earl of Northumberland. This Percy thought a deal of himself, she decided, and could cozen anyone to anything, except herself. Jealous as she was of anyone who took Everard away from her even for a little while, she scanned the other, Robert

Catesby, unfavourably, handsome as he was, with a sweetly curved mouth, broad spreading hands, and a candid pair of eyes that made every man trust him and do whatever he said. The pair had been staying at the Lord Mordaunt in Turvey after taking the fashionable waters at Bath; and Everard in his generous way had said they must no longer stay at an inn. So here they were, and she must put up with it, and Everard and the two guests passed their days in riding out and hunting, and archery on the great lawn, and talk; talk far into the night, and after she herself was in her bed, lying wakeful, her husband would come in, gentle and cheerful as usual, and she dared make no complaint lest he thought her suspicious and mean. It was not that, she told herself; they might eat at Gothurst as long as they wanted; it was the taking away of Everard's attention that she minded, so that already there seemed to be hidden jests among the three of them, laughter and winks at some matter she did not understand and pretended not to heed. But she would be glad when they were gone, with their high-crowned hats firm on their heads and two good saddles beneath them.

If she had known, there was reason for fear. There came a day when Tom Percy was elsewhere and Everard and Catesby happened to be riding along a lonely road on the way back from Harrowden. There was nobody within sight or earshot and of a sudden Catesby laid his hand on Everard's bridle, and made him draw rein.

"What is it, Bob?" said Everard. By now he would do anything for this fellow, who had quickly become his dearest friend, such was Catesby's charm and a kind of disarming innocence with it. The candid eyes looked into Digby's and then Catesby drew his hand from the other's bridle, and dropped his eyelids so that he no longer watched his friend's face.

"I have a thing to tell you," he said, "but you must swear on the Gospels to reveal it to no man."

Everard raised his eyebrows. "My word is surely my bond," he was beginning, but Catesby stopped him with a swift gesture and he fell silent, already curious. "The matter is most grave," said Catesby. "No man's word is enough, honourable though he be. Swear on this book." And he brought out a little narrow volume bound in the skin of unborn lambs, imprinted with a crucifix. Everard could not behold it without emotion; the Primer might not be seen openly nowadays in England; men could be thrown into prison merely for possessing it. He put his hand on it, and swore as he was asked.

A gleam of triumph showed beneath Catesby's veiled lids. A man of Digby's wealth would be an unconscionable boon to the plan they had made. Part must, therefore, be revealed to him, but no more than he need know; indeed no single man in the plot knew everything. To Father Garnet he, Catesby, had already revealed the matter in confession, which meant it was safe. But Father Garnet had been horrified, and Everard, when he heard the part he was to know, looked grave enough, his handsome features losing all their laughter. Yet he had given his word now, on the book.

"The Catholics will rise for us all over England," said Catesby confidently. "The Littletons alone will bring a thousand men. We must seize the royal children, lest anything go amiss with the Prince of Wales; and declare Charles King or, it may be, the Lady Elizabeth Queen. She is at Combe Abbey, and if you would make it your part to abduct her, and to give us money meantime, it will be well."

"But what . . . why . . ."

In a small cold voice, Catesby related the plan that was, he said, almost perfected; they would blow up the King and the Parliament with gunpowder when it met on the fifth of November.

Everard was glad to see the pair go. He had agreed, in course of the visit, to he knew not what; he could not find it in him to resist Catesby. He still hoped that the plot would be the fellow of several others, half-baked and early discovered, as was the case with Markham's plot, also that of Cobham and Raleigh. But Raleigh still lay in the Tower for this cause, even though it was not proven that he had taken any active part, only that he had taken money. Money, that was what they wanted now; should he himself not help them? Had he not written already to Cecil about toleration, and received no reply? Yet the thought of such a mass murder was terrible. Perhaps it would not, after all, be accomplished. What of Kenelm? Dared he risk his son's future in such a gamble, if it should fail? But he had given his word, his plighted word. He could say nothing now, only wait and see.

That same month of October a guest rode into Gothurst, a very tall man with dark features named Guy Fawkes. He had open, winning manners; he had been born in York of a minor county family, and had served in Flanders. He and Everard presently left the fire, which crackled brightly in the autumn cold, and sought a further place where they might talk in secret. Certain words passed, and Everard heard himself saying: "Will not the powder have grown damp with its long lying below Parliament?" He had begun to shiver with cold, away from the fire.

Mary Digby was still troubled about her husband, even though the pair from Bath, and Fawkes, had left. Everard had grown morose and silent, scarcely speaking to her even while they were alone. Only Kenelm seemed to give him pleasure, and he spent much time watching the boy, teaching him tunes, whistling to him. For the first time since her marriage Mary wondered if there could be another woman. She looked at herself in the mirror daily; was she becoming worn and plain with the cares of the house, the bearing of the children? Was it her fault in any way, had she said or done anything to offend him? But to ask was of no avail; Everard simply told her there was nothing wrong; if he was preoccupied it concerned the new English regiment in Flanders, raised since the peace with Spain to fight the Dutch.

"The Dutch were our allies in the Queen's time," Mary said, hoping to attract him by her cleverness. "They have uprisen against their sovereign," Everard replied. "If all states did that, the world would be out of order." And she persuaded herself that it was, after all, the English regiment that occupied him; if he went away to join it it would break her heart.

Within himself Digby continued in torment. He blamed himself bitterly for having given his pledged word. He could only hope that the plot would come to nothing; he could not warn the King; such a measure would bring retribution on his friends, perhaps himself and his family. He comforted himself by remembering similar news of many wild ideas; a dozen years back it had been spread abroad that the Jesuits in Spain had persuaded two English Catholics to smear the Queen's saddle with mercury poison, so that when she touched it and later ate, she would die. There had been Essex' rebellion, in which Catesby and others now freed had taken part. There had been the Main Plot, the Bye Plot, others one now heard nothing of. It all stemmed from discontent. At times he went to confession to ease his burdened mind, when there was a priest near. But one and all counselled gentleness, acceptance, waiting. They could not possibly favour this plot about gunpowder; it was too horrible to describe and in honour Everard could not tell them.

If Everard had known, Father Garnet himself was in sore perplexity and his hope was the same as Digby's, that the matter would be forgotten. Under the stern rule of the Church he might not, could not, break the confessional seal to reveal Catesby's plan. He had asked advice from Rome and had received the answer he expected: the seal of the confessional was of greater importance than any passing thing and he must not betray it on pain of death. But it was hard to know, and not act. He prayed over the matter often and long, and went about his duties as he might.

That same month Everard and Mary rode beyond the turning leaves to White Webbs with Father Garnet; he had stayed with them for some weeks and now considered it safe to return to what had become almost his home. Anne Vaux greeted them warmly and they made some cheer together, and entertained Bob Catesby to Everard's joy; in presence of the man's charm he could not doubt him. Mary tried to forget her trouble and take comfort in her religion and her husband's; all of them were moved, as always, by the miracle of the Eucharist in a small dark room lit only by candles, with guards set to warn them of intruders. Despite his ruddy complexion, Father Garnet's bearded face as he raised the Host looked pale in the wan light; he might have been the suffering Christ. Everyone received Him with the awareness they always had that this might be the last time, or the last but one; sooner or later, they would be found out. One had to remember the martyrs and their deaths, and live from day to day.

The Digbys returned home; but Everard did not seem content to stay there. Next day he said to Mary: "We will go to Coughton, for the time."

"Coughton? Tom Throckmorton's house? But why?" It was a draughty old place, by far less comfortable than Gothurst with fires blazing.

"For the hunt."

"There is plenty of hunting here." She was bewildered; why, at this time of year, move elsewhere? Did she not keep him in enough comfort in their home? What ailed him?

He grew impatient. "If I say it will be done, it will be. Get your gear together, and bring the children, and we will go. I have paid the rent of it and that is all; do not concern yourself further."

It would be rough living, she thought; smoking chimneys, the kitchen too near, dead game on the table forever reeking of blood. But she said nothing more, lest she anger him. In the end she went off with their stuff, the children, the greyhounds in their great collars, and Everard's guns; Everard himself elected to stay to close up Gothurst, which bewildered Mary further. So confused was she that she left behind her new dark winter gown, and he had to bring it with him.

Father Garnet celebrated All Saints and All Souls with many attending, then came to them again at Coughton. He said the London house he had arranged to take was no longer safe; they had been warned of it, and that elsewhere there was unrest, but here in the Midlands it was still quiet.

On a wet dark evening in the first week of October, a small crooked man in dark clothes, with grey hair, had been seated in his study in Burghley House in the Strand, writing a letter. It was evident that he did not carry out this task easily, although the matter of it was clear in his mind and had

31

been so for two years, and he was a devoted writer of letters. But the characters themselves, in this case, must be made to seem as if someone else, perhaps a poorly educated person, had written them. A stilted d, an embarrassed g, a different slope to the whole, was sufficient to disguise the Earl of Salisbury's customary flowing hand. When it was finished he, who before ennoblement had been Robert Cecil, leaned back, surveying his handiwork with no change of expression on his lean smooth face. All his life he had made this a mask when seen, to hide the hurt the world might do him. It mocked at cripples. But the hazel eyes gleamed shrewdly beneath their thinly enquiring arched brows; this night would bring his plan to perfection, despite the peace with Spain.

He glanced again at the letter.

My Lord, out of the love I bear to some of your friends I have a care of your preservation, therefore I would advise you as you tender your life to devise some excuse to shift of your attendance at this Parliament . . . for though there may be no appearance of any stir yet I say they shall receive a terrible blow this Parliament and yet they shall not see who hurts them.

He had rewritten it several times and had destroyed the first drafts in the fire; now, it would serve. He sent for his secretary, Monck, whose name in such a context secretly amused him. The man entered silently as was his habit; he was a good servant. Salisbury sealed the letter plainly, having added no signature.

"Take this to Lord Monteagle at his wife's house in Hoxton. Let no one see you as you go."

The rain drizzled down outside the window; there would not be many out tonight. Levinus Monck nodded; he had been on many such errands for his master, and would hide his face in his cloak-collar on the way. That would be foul with mud tonight. Why did my Lord Monteagle choose to stay there in an old place long empty, instead of his comfortable house here in the Strand?

He set off, however, obedient and silent, so that Salisbury, listening, did not even hear him ride away. He himself made his way with his splay-footed gait to the room where his daughters were; their brother was at Cambridge and more apt to follow horses than keep to his books. Salisbury closed the door of the room behind him and took a moment to survey the scene: Frances was sewing, a candle beside her, while Catherine, the younger, a child still, was roasting Spanish chestnuts in the fire, a long-handled pair of tongs in her fragile hands. On hearing her father's step she turned, cheeks flushed with heat from the hearth, smiling joyously at sight of him. She was a hunchback like himself, and her birth had killed her mother.

"Are they good chestnuts?" he asked. Her eyes, which were his dead wife's, looked up at him trustingly. The two of them knew they were separate from the world. Catherine Cecil held out a chestnut and Salisbury took it in his long fine fingers, shelled it, still hot, and put it in his mouth. Of all his children he loved Catherine the best, and feared the world would be as cruel to her as it had been to him.

"I dine at Whitehall," he told them.

"My hearts, make such cheer as you may." He caressed Catherine's smooth hair, kissed Frances on the cheek, and went to change his clothes. These were as always dark; but the coat he put on was of Venice velvet, and over it he hung a new watch from Nuremberg, which fascinated him as all jewels did. He crammed gleaming rings on to his slender fingers where, as always, he wore his wedding ring. It was of garnets set in gold, and every time he looked at it he thought of his wife Bess, and of how he had loved her at sight. He had been afraid that she would have objections to his person, but she had not; and they had been happy together for all too brief a time. But in the mirror now he saw only what he was accustomed to see, a solitary hunchback with arched brows and a secret face.

Monck did not have to enter the house in Hoxton; he met a footman of my lord's across the road. He gave the man the letter, and rode back without incident; as his master had foreseen, few were about.

The footman took the letter to young Lord Monteagle, whose title had lately been recognized after some delay. The young man opened it, stared at it and presently, deliberately, beckoned Tom Ward, one of the servants who waited in the room.

"This hand is vile," he said. "Help me to read it, I pray you." He was always courteous to his servants. Ward read it, puzzled: the letters seemed clear enough, why had my lord called him?

"I will ride out," said Monteagle then. He seemed ill at ease. The servant Ward spoke up. "On such a night, my lord, and your supper ready?"

"It will keep. Tell them to bank the fires. I must go."

Monteagle then took horse, supperless, and flogged his muddy way to Whitehall. He did not see the King, who was elsewhere enjoying his preferred country living. Monteagle instead was ushered into the presence of my Lord Salisbury and his elegant company; Suffolk, Northampton, the rest. Salisbury glanced at the letter, then drew Monteagle aside into a smaller room.

"This was begotten either of sport or frenzy," he said lightly. "I will acquaint the King when he returns. Meantime betake you to your rest."

My lord rode back then to his supper, but could not forbear over the next few days acquainting his friends with the news, as did the servant Ward. Some days later my lord made known to one Wintour the contents of the letter; next morning Wintour rode hard to White Webbs. Robert Catesby was there, making great stir with meetings of folk to the distress of Mistress Anne, who said it would get her house noticed. Fortunately Father Garnet was no longer in residence, having gone to Coughton to the Digbys, who had lately removed there with their house-furniture.

The King returned from hunting in course and was shown the letter. He glanced at it, then at Salisbury's expressionless face. This would be some doing of my lord's, he did not doubt; yet a good servant, and his little beagle was such, should be trusted so far. "My little beagle, my parrot," he murmured, knowing very well how greatly both names irked the new earl. The King spread his dirty white fingers against his slobbering mouth. His sad dark eyes, his mother's, grew vague beneath their hooded lids, then James chuckled suddenly. "I do not doubt ye have it all in hand, parrot," he said again. Suddenly his aspect changed to one of terror as a thought struck him.

"The fifth! The fifth of November! That is a Tuesday, the day Parliament meets. God save us, man, the fifth is a fell day for me. My father of blessed memory was done to death on that date, and I myself suffered mony things frae the Gowries, again on the fifth, a Tuesday also. Prosecute matters swiftly, my lord; make no delay in arresting these plotters; not a one maun be let go."

Two days later the Yorkshireman named Guy Fawkes, formerly an officer in the Low Countries, visited a certain cellar beneath the Painted Chamber in the House of Commons. He inspected some barrels that had lain there all year along with coal, iron bars and firewood; and came away with his tall soldierly figure erect, his dark face calm.

Everard sat in the inn at Dunchurch as

had been agreed with Catesby, with others of the same allegiance, playing cards. He stared at the black and red kings and queens and aces, trying to focus his thoughts on the game they were playing, while avoiding that deeper game in which his feet no longer touched the ground. He was already trapped and bewildered, obeying orders that in the ordinary way would have horrified him. He had ordered gunpowder, and had persuaded himself it was for the English regiment in Flanders, but knew in his heart it was not. It should arrive tonight, the gunpowder. There must be more elsewhere, perhaps nearby the house in London which Tom Percy said he had rented last year; it was near the Parliament. They had had hunting today and now, with the cards, were drinking wine. His kin and neighbours were here, his brother George, the Littletons whom he had known since childhood. A voice which seemed to have been heard long ago, in another life, whispered in his mind's ear that the Littletons could provide a thousand men. And this meeting tonight, the fifth of November, what would it lead to? There had been many others, all leading to nothing. He himself had got drunk so that the fumes of wine in his brain befuddled him and almost made him forget this morning at Coughton, with Kenelm's strong little arms close about his neck and the child's voice saying again and again, "Not go, not go."

But Everard had gone. The hunt had been furious and had lasted all day, and they had got a stag; the excitement had made him forget, for a time, how full he was of trouble when 'he took leisure to think. Now that he was seated on a bench and not the saddle thoughts pervaded him, making him play badly: he tried to thrust them away and concentrate on the game, but it was too late; he had lost.

"Ill fortune, Everard," said Humphrey Littleton. He was a fine-featured man in his forties, celebrated for never saying or doing a dishonest thing. That he was here tonight cheered Everard somewhat; they had been bidden here by Catesby under cover of a horse-meeting, and the hunt. There was some matter remaining in Everard's mind about the Princess Elizabeth; the child was at Combe Abbey nearby and he awaited instructions. Instructions! How did Catesby manage to instruct so many who were not in the ordinary way fools? Yet here they were: it was another foregathering such as Mistress Anne had complained of at White Webbs, making her house notable. An inn would take less harm.

There were sounds of arrival outside and presently Catesby himself came in. He was pale, and looked round them for a moment as if to assess how many there were and deciding it was not enough. Everard flung down his cards.

"What's amiss, Bob?" It was time they had it out in the open; all this coming and going for obscure purposes was foreign to him, and no doubt also to the rest. Catesby spread his hands in the way he had, then made a short statement. The King and Salisbury were dead, he said; he did not relate how. In some manner Everard found he could not believe him. But some did. His own escape from the card-table was covered by the entry of more men, greeting the rest as friends. The card-game would not now be played to a finish; but the other?

"How did they die? Is it certain?"

Catesby beckoned Everard aside into one of the smaller chambers of the low-ceilinged inn; both tall men had to stoop to pass the lintel. The room seemed no bigger than a box, their two selves filling it. "Tell me of it," said Digby. "Tell me."

Catesby stared, his features working, and Everard had the certainty that he too was deeper into matters than he had foreseen. Or was he in fact enjoying the proceedings as a man might do in a play, with himself making the speeches? Maybe. Everard felt cold doubts rise; the news had been too pat.

"I do not believe it," he was beginning, when Catesby suddenly erupted into easy speech. It behoved, he said, all Catholics to act together now; they would be out after them already, in the shires.

"They will down us if they may," he mouthed, when from the other room a babble of sound spread; the news had been told, and no man knew what to do next. Catesby stumbled out, Everard after him; there was turmoil everywhere, they were saying, confusion in the State, crowds swarming in London. "We must not stay here," called Catesby, raising his voice above the din. "Let us get to Warwick; bring all your arms, and bid the servants bring horses, for we will need them all."

Everard felt a touch on his arm. He spun about to behold Humphrey Littleton, his fine face drawn with distaste.

"I am no longer of this allegiance," he said squarely. "I will go back whence I came, and hope that my absence was not noted. Do you the same, for there is only one place to where this shouting and stir will lead; the Tower and the gallows."

But Everard looked at the other faces of those he knew, and could not bring himself to desert them. He heard Littleton ride off, and rejoined his neighbours in the main room. Whether the news were true or false, they would not now be left in peace; and Catesby was his friend, and he loved him.

At Warwick Castle he knew he was on the wrong side of the law; several folk had refused to join them, and the stables were broken open and horses taken; Everard heard himself giving the commands in a dream; he, a horse-thief! Many were beginning to look grim and downcast; what was all the pother, and where were they going? Robert Wintour came to Everard and tried to dissuade him as Littleton had done. "It is against the law," he said. The stamping and clinking of saddle-armour could be heard nearby.

"Some of us may not look back." They took horse: by now they were almost like disembodied folk, ghosts riding always through the cold November night. They were still on the way at three in the morning of the sixth of November, 1605.

"We can escape to some port. You, Digby, have money; I saw the rent-bag come." It was true enough; one of his servants, who still rode behind, had brought the rents while they sat at cards. By now they were no more than a useless weight. They would not reach a port. After that Catesby grew less friendly; he set men about the rest with pistols, in order that they might not slink off. They rode all that day, spending the night fully clad at Wintour's house of Huddington in Oxfordshire. Catesby forced his host to write a letter. "You must ask for aid," he said. "With your writing it will seem better than the spoken word."

"Well, sirs, this letter will be enough to hang me," replied Wintour, but he wrote it unwillingly, and sent it off with one of the men. By now despair had settled on most of the party, except that Catesby continued oddly jolly, as if triumph of some kind awaited him. But the greater number with them now were servants, with Digby, a man named Grant, Tom Percy and the younger Littleton. Despite their vigilance more men escaped into the woods as they rode.

There had been a priest in hiding at Huddington and that morning they had heard Mass and received the Sacrament. It was the last comfort they were to have. Digby rode now as if he were fevered, dreaming dreams. His thighs were saddle-sore, he the huntsman. Where was he going now? What of the hopes for Kenelm? He dared not think of Kenelm now, or of Mary.

Despite the watch John Littleton left the party and went back to surrender himself to the sheriff at Huddington. His brother had already gone. It would avail them nothing; both would be condemned. But their going convinced Everard that he too must make a bid for escape. He knew the woods here, nearing Holbeach. There was a dry pit where he and his servants might hide with their horses, and later, when the hue and cry had died, go abroad. The folk had not been for them on the way; they had cried always that they were for King James.

Riding, riding; the thud of tired hooves on dead leaves. There was another sound coming now; they were after him. For a time he outraced them, thinking to get himself, if worse befell, to the magistrate's house at Dudley and give himself up there. But they burst through the thinned trees and surrounded him, him and his men. Digby curvetted his horse, making it rear with flailing hooves. "Here he is," they cried, "here he is."

"Here he is indeed," Everard called out, having tried to frighten them with the curvetting and rearing of his horse, whom he controlled absolutely. But such antics were in vain; they were closing about him, and it was useless now to try to reach the pit. He let his tired horse down; he had been three days in the saddle. He saw a group of implacable, hostile, unknown faces. They neared and surrounded him, and took his sword. Two of his servants had refused to leave him and they were also taken.

The others had drawn rein at Holbeach, and there a worse fate awaited them; some of the gunpowder had grown damp, and they left it to dry by the fire. A spark caught it while they were resting, and the powder exploded. Grant was blinded and some others badly burned. The sound of the explosion had torn at the servants' ragged nerves and they escaped, most of them, before the law caught them yet awhile. Master and servant now were filled with fear.

The Sheriff's men rode in at Holbeach and there was no defence put up except for three shots, one hitting a tree. If Catesby had hoped for reward in the whole matter he received only a bullet for it; he and Tom Percy were at once shot dead by two from the same rifle, and whatever tale they had to tell would never now be told. A third man died and before he was cold, they had stripped off his boots to get his silk stockings. The rest, shocked, burned, bewildered, were taken; not one man among them could piece together the whole tale.

Kenelm would never forget the silence in the house. Not one of the sounds came now that he had grown used to day after day; Johnny's gurgling—he had been taken elsewhere—the halloo of the hunt setting off and returning daily; the tramp of his father's high soft riding-boots as he strode into the nursery to toss Kenelm up in his arms at last and ask what he had done with his day. His kindly and comforting voice had gone, and his laughter; there was no laughter now. Somewhere, once, there was a woman sobbing, and nobody explained why. Once, also, at last, a woman in black came in; Kenelm's mother, her face changed dreadfully into a white mask with reddened eyes. Mary moved stiffly, like an old woman. She came to where Kenelm was and stood looking down at him, and yet through him; he began to be very much afraid.

"They have taken your father and

condemned him like a common criminal. They will bring him out and hang him, then cut him down and cut him open. They will cut his parts from him and burn them in the fire. They have left us few goods and no fair name. I know well enough what they were after now; money, lands, but not only that; they wanted to make the name of Catholics detested up and down the land. They wanted to blame them for a devilish plot so base that it would never be forgotten, and its anniversary has been proclaimed by the King to be held every year in thanksgiving that he and his escaped. I and mine have not. They cried out when your father came into court that he was the goodliest man there, but that will not spare him. I have been a fool, a fool; I should have stopped it all at the beginning; I should never have had Catesby in my house."

She talked on, and Kenelm felt the sobs rising in his throat in a kind of bewilderment, and cried out presently while she was still talking.

"Where is my father?" he asked. "Where is he?"

"At a rope's end." And she turned and

walked away to the window, and stood looking out unseeing at the bleak lands about Coughton, and thought suddenly of Gothurst that she had been allowed to keep: that, and one-third of her income. They had taken everything else; she was poor now like other recusants. It never occurred to her for an instant to abandon the Catholic faith. The fines would be paid while she had money to pay them, and by now that meant ten pounds a month for every servant as well. Like the rest, she was forbidden to appear at Court or live within ten miles of London. Her house might be broken into and searched on a magistrate's warrant at any time. Any Protestant who entertained her or her Catholic servants would be fined. If she tried to educate her son abroad—there was no hope for his promotion at home—he would be declared an outlaw. He would have no right to inherit lands by marriage. If she were found to possess a crucifix they would mutilate the figure.

Kenelm tried to imagine his father at a rope's end, but the image would not come. It was as well. When Everard was in fact executed, the rope was cut before it had time to strangle him and he fell from the gallows, gashing open his forehead on the wooden platform. He was conscious during what followed; near the end, after his parts had been cut off and burned in the fire and his body carved open and its bowels dragged to the flames, the executioner ripped out his heart at last, and, holding it up still bleeding, intoned: "This is the heart of a traitor."

"Thou liest," replied Digby in a clear voice, then died. The crowd swayed and murmured in amazement.

Father Garnet was discovered and taken, later; and the faithful lay-brother Nicholas Owen, Little John. When the time came to torture the old man for questioning he showed them his rupture; they knew well enough it was against the law that such a man should be stretched on a rack. But they put an iron corset on him, and racked him then; but his bowels gushed out and he died in great agony. Father Garnet they hanged, later; but that time the crowd called: "Hold, hold," when they would have cut the rope, and the priest was allowed to die by hanging before the rest was done. They said an ear of wheaten straw splashed with his blood, rescued for a relic, congealed into a likeness of his suffering face. After that the King and Salisbury rested from persecutions for a while, turning their attention to other things. Salisbury had only seven years to live. At the end, swollen with dropsy, and a great tumour, he was heard to cry out: "O Lord Jesus, now, sweet Jesus, let me come to Thee . . . my audit is made, I am safe, I am safe."

The King lived on.

2

THE silence, and his terror, had an outward effect on Kenelm also; it made him noisy. For the rest of his life he would justify everything he did with great bragging, whether by the word or the pen. When he was old enough he was given the letters his father had written to him from the Tower on the eve of his execution. Of this one thing Kenelm never spoke. He carried the letters about with him all his life and his servant saw him reading them often. He knew by then that his father had recited *Domine, dirige me* on the climb to the scaffold; but it hadn't happened, the rope had been too soon cut, and it left in Kenelm a great uncertainty.

About this time, to his outrage, he fell ill with "a great and dangerous sickness". He had never before lacked the physical strength to raise himself from his bed; he lay there languid and sweating for days and weeks, while his bones grew long. When he was a man he would be very tall;

after the illness, when his full strength had returned, he looked already older than he was, larger than his age, with the vital mane of hair that soon earned him recognition wherever he went. He was no longer Everard Digby's son; he was himself. But he remembered the verses his father had written before they dragged him on a hurdle to St. Paul's.

> Who's that which knocks? O stay,
> my Lord, I come;
> I know that call, since first it made
> me know
> My self, which makes me now with
> joy to run
> Lest he be gone that can my duty
> show.

Kenelm would become a poet also, in time. In time many things would happen to him. Meantime he regarded the world with some caution, amid his curiosity: familiar things were welcome, and strange things a challenge to the mind.

About the age of seven, he fell in love.

"Now you crown me King and then I will

crown you Queen of the Isle of Man."

The large curly-headed child spoke earnestly in what was already a gruff voice. The beautiful young girl, three years older, seemed his junior. There was often fact behind Kenelm's fantasies; Venetia Anastasia Stanley was in fact descended, on her father's side, from the Earls of Derby who had long ruled Man. In the two children's hands were shaky wreaths they had made from the flowers growing round them in the fields and woods; lady's-smock, daisies, bugle, cowslips, eyebright, buttercup, clary. Kenelm had twined in oak and yew twigs as well from the trees in the great north avenue at Gothurst, and thereafter they had wandered together back into the sun, with Johnny trailing behind with the two girls and taking no part in their game. Kenelm knelt now on the grass and felt Venetia's cool fingers set the crown on his head; then he placed his wreath on hers and kissed her. He was fond of kissing Venetia. In fact each child was somewhat lonely; Kenelm could never find Johnny good company, and Venetia lived mostly with her governess and her father's tenants, her mother being dead and Sir Edward Stanley a solitary man devoted to his books.

"You have disarranged my hair, you and your crown," she said. But the wreath stayed in place and they sat back and looked at one another, liking what they saw. Kenelm smoothed Venetia's bright brown hair where it lay on her shoulders; she wore no ruff today and had been allowed to come just as she was, with her long throat and bright head bare and free. It happened almost every day since she had been brought from Shropshire to Enston Abbey nearby. It did not matter whether her father, Sir Edward Stanley, were at home or not; he devoured books in his library and mostly left his daughter alone. Suddenly she remembered with joy that he had promised to take her to Court, and started to speak of it straight away because Kenelm always understood.

"I shall see the Princess's wedding to the County Palatine after Yule. And Yule itself will be grand. They say the Palatine is not good enough for Princess Elizabeth and that the Queen is angry, for she wanted to see her daughter Queen of

Spain." All this tattle she had picked up from the servants and tenants, and he listened somewhat incuriously. Venetia was so beautiful she did not need to talk. Her cheeks were the exact colour of damask roses. He would be sad when she went away. She must not go; must not leave him, ever.

Venetia talked on. "And of course I shall wear my hair on a high frame, as that's the fashion; and a farthingale."

"Do not wear one of those!" He was horrified; to bind up Venetia's beautiful hair in a stiff ugly way, and a monstrous farthingale hiding her slenderness! The blood rushed to his face with his earnest temper; he suddenly remembered that he could not be there with her, and his face fell.

"I would I could come there," he said, "but we are out of favour."

"So are we. My grandfather is still in the Tower." That was the Earl of Northumberland, imprisoned since the time of the Gunpowder Plot for suspected complicity, but in fact he had been too powerful a rival for the late Earl of Salisbury to endure and it was a convenient way to be rid of him, and they had levied a huge fine.

"Perhaps everybody is out of favour," said Venetia, and giggled. She saw that Kenelm was still downcast, remembering his father, and said quickly, to reassure him: "Have no fear, the King will receive you one day when you have performed some mighty deed. But don't turn into one of the pretty boys who hang round his neck." She was back at the tenants' gossip again. Kenelm laughed suddenly and so did she. If he were to hang about the King's neck his size alone would bring that monarch down to the ground. They both knew it and rocked and shouted with laughter accordingly, the flowers on their heads shaking and some falling off, into Venetia's plain linen lap. She took a flower and began twisting it in her fingers. They fell silent again; there was always the journey from silence to laughter, between them, then silence once more;

"May I kiss you again?" he asked suddenly. She smiled, and let him touch her smooth cheek with his warm eager lips. He adored her; her flesh was like the flowers they had picked, fragrant and delightful, and her mouth had a sweet curve even in repose. He wished that he could tell her in the words of a poet how beautiful she was; perhaps when he went to Oxford, which was to happen soon, he would manage it, being by then learned.

"Whenever we are apart, I will write to you," he said. "Will you answer, or will you be too busy enjoying the Court?" He still felt sad at thought of that parting; but Venetia's mind had already returned there, like a butterfly. They said the most beautiful woman at Court was the young Countess of Essex, but Venetia's admirers —and various gentlemen had already showed an interest in her and she had rebuffed none—said she herself was more so. It would remain to be seen, and life in any case was delightful, if sometimes lonely. Venetia moved her slender body where she sat on the grass, and Kenelm reached over and straightened her crown, which had fallen awry. "Yours is over one eye," she reminded him, and set it straight in her turn. It was pleasant to be here in the Buckinghamshire sunshine and be admired even by someone as young as Kenelm. How young he really was! She remembered it as he took her hand and let it rest in his. He was only a child, playing a game, she thought; it was not like the others.

Mary Digby, passing by one of the great mullions of Gothurst, observed the pair sourly. It would be a good thing when that little minx Venetia Stanley was sent to Court. Mary's mouth tightened; she was no longer the happy girl who had bared her white feet on pilgrimage in the Welsh valleys. To maintain the Faith, pay fines and mourn one's husband left little pleasure and she felt none now at sight of the two young people on the grass. The thought came to her that Kenelm should be taken out of the way even before he went to Oxford. If only John Digby, his uncle, would take the boy, young as he was, with him on some diplomatic mission abroad! One never knew where John was going next, for he was in favour and could speak foreign languages. It would be good for Kenelm. She would write, as soon as might be, and ask John concerning it.

Standing there, she watched her son with Venetia Stanley and remembered a grudge she had against the child's father.

It was unimportant, but in general Sir Edward Stanley was a man she would not trust; he had been known to inform, long ago, concerning a supposed Jesuit plot to poison the old Queen by smearing mercury on her saddle. There had been one such plot after another talked of, but now they were done. Aye, now they were done; there would be no more in her generation.

The sun went in and Venetia was taken home.

"What a fine road" Kenelm shouted against the wind. It stung his cheeks and brought tears to his eyes and whipped at the plume in his hat of the new fashion, turned up at one side and worn bravely with one's hair flying beneath. And there was the sea itself, glittering! He had seen it at last! How wide it was, and how magnificent, belonging to all the oceans of the world! It was as if one could see to the end of place and time; beyond the chalk cliffs lay the world, everything.

His kinsman John Digby smiled, his pleasant worried face relaxing. He was pleased that the boy was enjoying the journey. He himself had been glad to help poor Mary when she asked, for he knew in private that he had helped to destroy Mary's husband, without meaning to; it was he who had ridden from Sir John Harington, who had charge of the Princess Elizabeth at Combe Abbey, that time about the news they had there of the Gunpowder Plot and the plan to seize the Princess and perhaps make her Queen. Well, Everard had paid the price of that; and now this son of his was promising, full of life and asking questions about everything: his cousin had even managed to teach him a little Spanish already, and they would learn more on the voyage. Sir John —he had been knighted by King James only a few years ago, after rising high in the estimation of that royal lover of handsome male good looks, not that there had been anything dishonourable, and Sir John's good wife waited patiently at home —Sir John pondered on this Spanish visit, which he had made before. He heard the sound of their horses' hooves pound the good flat Dover Road, and presently they came to a sight of the King's own charter ship riding in the Roads in the late August sunshine, and he pointed it out to Kenelm.

He was unprepared for the boy's tremendous and devouring delight. It was the first time Kenelm Digby had seen the sea and a ship, and he promised himself it would not be the last; how beautiful she was, rocking at anchor with her sails furled and while the light waves glittered about her! He could not wait to get aboard her.

He shouted something of it to his kinsman, and saw Sir John make a wry mouth. "Wait till you are in the Bay, and you may not care so greatly for sea-travel." But the older man was in fact thinking already of the tricky diplomacy of his mission; to succeed where he had failed before. Last time he had been instructed to arrange a Spanish marriage for the Prince of Wales, and had been fobbed off insultingly with a half-promise of a younger Infanta of six. This time it would be different. Spain was known by now to have her difficulties, even despite the peace; Dutch pirates swarmed upon her coasts and sold foreign goods, even counterfeit coin, in exchange for silver from the Americas. "They will come to an end of all that one day, and then where is their power?" mused Sir John, but he did not say it aloud. He allowed himself to join in his young kinsman's enthusiasm, and almost felt as young as Kenelm again: otherwise, he was thirty-seven. They spurred their mounts and rode on down into the port, the servants with the baggage following placidly behind on their slower beasts. Their masters had brought enough with them to satisfy the requirements of the new Court of Madrid, no more; a few shirts, hose embroidered with silver and soft boots for riding, satin shoes for dancing, guns for the shoot if King Philip III should invite them; all such necessaries, but little to spare.

Kenelm explored every corner of the great ship, from its scrubbed decks with cannon gleaming dully in the sun down to the smallest cabin in the dark hold. There were no women on board, and he knew a sudden, unexpected relief from the surveillance of his mother. Henceforth he would lead his own life, and Venetia—he had sent her off some lines before sailing—should be part of it. He listened to the wind in the high shrouds and the cracking of the flag of England flung out at last on the breeze, when they were under way; and knew that some time, somehow, he would have his own ship, and would sail beyond these coasts to a great adventure, of what sort he was not yet certain. But he felt the decks shift beneath his straddled feet with the sea's roll, and was happy; Sir John kept to his cabin, writing despatches. The crew answered back the huge curly-headed English boy with their ready salt wit, and told him what he wanted to know about the compass and the stars; when night fell he was still gazing at these, until he was sent for to sleep. He went down with a memory of Orion, and his Dog, blazing up there, and Venus like a golden pear-drop, low in the heavens. He had looked for his own Crab sign but it was not visible, and clouds covered the moon. He undressed and relieved himself and got into his bunk, and slept dreamlessly.

He was less enchanted with Spain when it came. He had thought of a land of gleaming riches and martial history, whereas all there were, as far as one could see, and after the bustle of the port, were boulders looking as if they had been tumbled down by hungry giants who had mistaken them for bread; and a harsh sky the colour of copper, and, in course, dry brown sierras past the half-deserted villages. "Why are they so empty?" he asked his kinsman, and the latter motioned to him to lower his voice. They had entered a coach on landing and it rocked with the pot-holes and ruts they met; brown dust was everywhere and the mules, to which the coach was harnessed, moved so slowly Kenelm wanted to get out and drive them himself and make them work faster. "There was, some years ago, a plague and famine everywhere, and with the lack of any harvest the peasants fled from their debts to the towns," he was told. "In those you will see many beggars."

"That is sad." One saw beggars, it was true, in towns in England; but not like these swarms that clustered about the carriage whenever it stopped at some inn on the road; thin brown starved folk, with haggard faces and great dark eyes in their heads that seemed as if they looked on doom. "Does not the King help them?" Kenelm asked. At home they would have received help, in the parishes. Sir John frowned again.

"Moderate your tongue; we may be overheard and reported on. You must observe everything you see, but do not comment on it openly; wait till you are alone with me, and otherwise hold your peace." He himself was reflecting on a recent discovery he had made of Spanish pensions paid over the years to sundry Englishmen who included the late Lord Salisbury. It made him, briefly, impatient with his young kinsman: he wanted peace to think.

So Kenelm, for once, remained silent and noted everything that passed; he found it an interesting exercise. At last they came to a town which was at the same time gleaming and full of shadows, the King of Spain's new capital of Madrid, below the Guadarramas. They rode up to a forbidding long wall and entered by a small door, and thence by corridors to an ornate room where on a throne sat a man who was evidently the King of Spain, but to Kenelm's eye had nothing notable about him except his upturned moustaches. Philip III greeted Sir John Digby passively; they might never have met before. The talk was dull and uniform; soon the King turned for relief to old Calderón, who stood near, as if to beg him to make conversation; the man in power, the Duque de Lerma, was not here today and Philip felt his mind grow blank. "His two passions," Kenelm was told by Sir John afterwards, "are religion and the hunt. He did not leave the latter even to attend the Queen's funeral when she died in childbirth. He is a man who dislikes altering his habits in any way."

"That would seem a pity."

"What do you know of it, boy? You see only a glittering Court which dictates fashions to Europe still, as in the days of its glory. You do not see the bankruptcy, the despair."

There had been however a young man slightly older than Kenelm himself at Court, the King's son the young Prince of the Asturias, heir to the throne. He was somewhat vapid in appearance; had fair hair and a lower lip which jutted out incredibly, and Kenelm had tried a few words of Spanish on him learnt during the journey. The Prince's eyes, which resembled those of a prawn, turned on him briefly and held a gleam of unaccustomed interest before it died. "Do you like paintings?" the Prince asked Kenelm, who floundered a little.

"I like all such things, Highness, in especial anything new."

The Prince bowed as if to conclude the conversation, and Kenelm noticed that he was wearing the *golilla*, the new high collar that was soon to replace the ruff; this was a measure for economy taken by many of the courtiers, as the Court like everything else in the country was greatly in debt. Nothing, however, seemed to be spared in the way of magnificent outer clothing, which glistened with gold and silver embroidery, velvet and soft leather. The Prince of the Asturias beckoned Kenelm, and took him over to where a group of young ladies stood, dressed stiffly but chattering together in low voices. "This is the Señor Digby," said the Prince in Spanish; a dark-eyed girl extended her white hand and Kenelm kissed it. He admired the Princess's looks as though he had, indeed, been a painter; she wore a green satin train figured with gold, and above it her dark curls were trimmed formally, like a hedge. To his relief she was French, and so he could talk to her. To the stiff, anxious Court Isabel of Bourbon brought gladness and relief; she was a daughter of Henri IV and had inherited much of her murdered father's charm without, Kenelm noted, the famous stink of that monarch's unwashed armpits. But the scent of musk and amber and incense was stronger in any case here than the sweat of folk. The Prince of the Asturias followed his Princess with his light-lashed eyes, as well he might, and soon Kenelm knew his own talk with Isabel was at an end; but she seemed happy enough in Spain.

He remembered Venetia and how much he had to write to her; but it was as though all life and movement had stopped here long ago on the death of England's enemy, Spain's implacable Philip II; now it was like a place in an enchanted forest, sleeping for a hundred years. He said so to Sir John when they were again alone.

"It is true enough," said the diplomat. "Everyone thinks the supply of silver from the Americas to be inexhaustible, but as

70

matters stand I doubt if our King is justified in hoping for sixty thousand as a dowry if the Infanta marries our Prince of Wales."

"I could not stay here for long. I am stifled. There is too much etiquette."

"Why, you will never make an ambassador if you say that, Kenelm. Would it please you to study for a little while at one of the universities? Salamanca is famous, and the lectures are in Latin so you will not be at a loss."

"I would like that very well. I long to be with living people again. And I can learn Spanish."

"Well, it shall be done; I myself have some few matters to conclude before we go home, and when it is time for that I will send for you."

So Kenelm prepared to journey to Salamanca, with the plume in his hat flourishing. He was pleased with himself; had travelled now, had made his obeisance at Court, had handled the Spanish counterfeit money that was ruining the economy, and also the double-stamped *vellon* with which the King's advisers had tried to stop the ensuing disease of inflation while only making it worse. It would be pleasant—he admitted it to himself—to be free of Sir John and his constant admonitions; he himself could say what he liked in Salamanca.

But when the posts came from England Kenelm was disappointed, the feeling crowding out his pleasure; there was no word yet from Venetia, and he had written to her several times.

Used as she had been all her life to the quiet of the country with no greater sound than horses' hooves and lambs bleating, Venetia was at first dazzled and bewildered, even sickened, by the noise, glitter and stench of the Court; then she began to enjoy it, for with her beauty she was noticed at once. It was no longer dangerous to court Northumberland's granddaughter now my lord of Salisbury was dead. The gentlemen in their great padded breeches in imitation of His Majesty, who feared swords, thronged about her; and the women in their gross farthingales, which were known to be an aid in secret pregnancy, envied her. She dressed herself like them; and like them had her bodices cut so low that one's bosom was almost revealed as was totally the fashion in France. The ruff was no longer so uncomfortable as it had been in the old Queen's day, but following Spain fanned out behind the head like the exotic white tail of a swimming fish.

It was difficult to keep linen clean because of the fogs and the smoke from fires of sea-coal which everyone in town had lit in their houses and lodgings; but the maids starched and laundered valiantly, and Venetia kept herself clean with rosewater and used amber and musk, very expensive, to combat the stink of sweat even from the most genteel of persons; the King himself stank and so did most others. As for beauty, Venetia had no need to paint herself with red and white lead as some did; her admirers wrote bad verse on the theme of her skin, her hair, her discretion, her gentle voice, her bright hazel eyes, everything she did or was believed to do. Later a verse would be pinned to the door of her lodging. *Pray come not near. For Dame Venetia Stanley dwelleth here.*

Her first night at Court she would

always remember; looking about her she saw the padded throng, the King and Queen on their thrones, the Queen's blonde hair piled up and her clear skin visited with pimples from rich living; she had painted to hide them. By contrast, a very beautiful young woman stood near, eyeing a tall fair man with a short beard, who waited near the King. The girl stood idly, her lower lip pouting a little, her hair radiant in the candlelight, her bosom half bare; the lovely Countess of Essex, of whom Venetia had already heard. Drop pearls hung from the lobeless, degenerate ears; despite her beauty there were not many near her except one dark young man, who watched her always. He was tall, and looked like an athlete. As Venetia passed by to make her curtsey the Countess's cool eyes assessed her. She does not like me, the girl thought; and where was my Lord Essex that he did not have an eye to his wife?

Venetia was presented to the King and Queen. James at first disgusted her, for even at a slight distance one could smell his odour, still like that of mice in damp straw. His weak legs would not support

74

him and when he rose it was to lean on the shoulder of the fair bearded young man, whom he called Robin. The Queen spoke to Venetia kindly enough, in a mixture of Scots and Danish; it was difficult to understand her, but all she expected, evidently, was a nod of agreement and a smile, so Venetia gave it, and passed on amid the crowd.

There was dancing presently, and as Venetia watched she saw the tall young man with dark hair approach Frances Essex and take her hand to lead her out. They smiled at one another and before Venetia was able to watch further she herself was led on to the floor, and began to enjoy herself. Excited and laughing, she was twirled about the great room in the dances she had been taught well enough at Enston Abbey and in Shropshire, to both of which places a dancing-master had come; the branle, the galliard, the slow pavon. Once the fair young man who had supported the King came to her, for James had resumed his seat, and was presented as Robert Carr, Viscount Rochester. His eyes rested hotly on Venetia as his arm encircled her waist and they began to

dance. The fiddles sounded almost un-
heard amid the stamping and leaping of
the great measure of the galliard.

"What folly all this is, even with one as
lovely as yourself," he murmured. "I
would sooner be on a good horse,
following the hunt, or letting my dogs
follow me. Will you be at the hunt the day
after tomorrow? The King rides to Theobalds, and I with him, and we could meet
one another again then."

Venetia shook her head, smiling; Dad
had paid for the London lodging, but he
would not be best pleased if she travelled
to Theobalds and demanded that as well,
unless she were invited to stay with the
royal party. She said something of it and
Robert Carr grew eager. "I have only to
ask the King," he said, "and you shall be
included. Come with us, for it will be a
great pleasure to me to see you in the
saddle and ride by you."

His voice was like a boy's, but rougher,
with traces of a Scots accent. She learned
later that he had attracted the King's
attention at a tournament, where Carr had
been unhorsed and had fallen and broken
his leg. "The King was very kind to me

then," he said. "I owe him much," and he gave a little grimace, thinking no doubt of his new title and the way he had earned it. Venetia saw, over his shoulder, the Countess of Essex freed again from the embrace of the Prince of Wales, the young athletic-seeming man with dark hair, who had had to lead out the wife of an ambassador and so must leave his mistress. Venetia saw Frances Howard's eyes fixed on herself, full of cold dislike. Venetia shivered a little. I would not like to have her as an enemy, she thought. Does she covet my partner? She made herself speak, to forget the incident.

"Lady Essex is very beautiful," she told Rochester. He smiled like a cat with a secret herring.

"Not more so than you, my beauty," he told her, and one hand began to fondle her breast. Venetia drew back angrily and tried to leave the floor and this forward partner. But Rochester was immediately abject.

"Forgive my rough manners," he said, "but your loveliness unmanned me."

There was no opportunity to answer, for the King called for his Robin. "Leave the lasses, my boy, and come and cheer old Dad. Here is a willing partner for your bonny young lady." And he thrust forward, with his soiled white hand, a slim, dark, older man, with sensitive features and a gentle aspect. "This is Tom Overbury, who will see ye round."

"You have done me an ill turn," muttered Rochester to Sir Thomas as he himself went perforce back to the King. But he had not spoken loudly and His Majesty was comforted, and began to fondle his Robin. Later Queen Anne herself joined in the *courante*, led out by her son, her tall majestic figure moving gracefully; it was said she loved dancing and the masque and had once even blacked her face to appear in one. All this and more Venetia heard from her new partner, who was a scholar and his talk reminded her of Kenelm, only not so boisterous; the thought suddenly came to her that she had not remembered Kenelm all evening.

"You are thoughtful," said Overbury. His voice had sad overtones, and she would have replied, but a third young man, somewhat short-legged and with large hands like a workman's, thrust between them and demanded her hand in the slow pavon. "This is Edward Sackville, brother to the Earl of Dorset," Overbury told her courteously, then took himself off. "Who hath nigh ruined himself with venery, sweetheart; I myself should be Earl soon," Sackville told her at once. He was the most richly dressed man in the hall, but she did not like him any more than she had liked Robin Carr: there seemed to be too many rakehelly men anxious to take advantage of a young maid newly at Court. But she listened to Sackville's talk, for always one learned something of the busy way of life here. In the end, unwillingly, he took Venetia back to her guardian, Mistress Islip, who had come with her and who sat by the wall.

Later Venetia was to be sorry she had not met the Prince of Wales, whether or not, as folk whispered, he was Lady Essex' lover. Not long afterwards he took a sweating sickness, and it was assumed it was a quartan fever and that he would recover; but he did not, and before his sister Elizabeth's wedding to the Count Palatine the year following, Prince Henry died and there was mourning at Court; some whispered that the Prince's own father had poisoned him.

"He would have made a better King than James ever has," remarked Ned Sackville, lounging at ease at last in Venetia's lodging; by now he had called there several times, and made himself at home; she began to like him better, his talk was amusing and one learnt more and still more of the happenings about Court. Everyone was bewildered now since the Prince's death; the next heir was little Prince Charles, whom nobody had met, for he was kept in the country. He was said to be backward and to have a stammer, and to have been unable to walk till he was seven.

"Also my Lady Essex hath lost an admirer," said Sackville blandly. "She will be able now to turn her greater attention to the King's Robin. They say she fancies him and hath done so for long. But I do not know what will come of it."

"Where is her husband?" asked Venetia, and Sackville laughed.

"Little innocent that you are! He is travelling abroad for his greater education. He is a stick of a young man, not like his father. They say that marriage was never consummated, as it took place when both were children. He may well arrive home in course to find that others have visited the nest before him."

Venetia felt a sudden longing for the country and Kenelm; this Court was not clean.

Yule passed, with its feasting; then there was the Princess's wedding, with grief for dead Prince Henry of Wales forgotten in the laughter of the bride, the grave devotion of her young German bridegroom, and the eagerness of King James to inspect the couple in their bride-bed on the morning after the marriage. For a time there was still rejoicing and holiday despite the known displeasure of the Queen. On a cold day in February, in the privy garden at Whitehall, two tall men walked, both wearing fur-lined cloaks against the chill wind from the river. One was Sir Thomas Overbury, the other Robert Carr, now Lord Rochester. They walked with arms linked, for they had been friends since Rochester's youth when they had met one another in Edinburgh. Now Rochester was the King's unofficial secretary as well as his love, there were constant queries which Overbury, the better scholar of the two, could always answer, whereas Rochester with his lack of wit could not. So far the King remained satisfied, loving well his pretty Robin and never suspecting that the answers on which Robin promised to ponder came from elsewhere.

"I will take the matter and think upon it, Sire."

"Ay, do so, that's my clever Robin, my pretty Robin."

Rochester at times wearied of it all, especially as by now he was the lover in fact as well as hope of Frances Essex, who pursued him relentlessly. Carr was flattered rather than in love; he had accepted Frances' body as a favour rather than as almost royal condescension from this niece of Northampton who was another man's wife. Already he was somewhat sated with her, and discussed the matter with Overbury; if Frances got her divorce because as she said her husband was impotent, should he himself marry her? Would it improve his fortunes?

"Never," said Overbury firmly. "Frances Essex is good enough as a mistress, no doubt, but never a wife."

They were passing a hawthorn tree, its branches bitter and bare. From beyond it stepped the figure of a small man, bowing, his unpleasant face carefully devoid of expression. There was no doubt that Northampton had overheard. Overbury flushed and they went on their way, having returned my lord's bow: from further off there came the sound of laughter, and the Princess, hand in hand with her German bridegroom, and attendants came out, Elizabeth's lovely face glowing under her fur hood. With her were several pretty women, as well as her devoted new husband. Frances Essex and Venetia Stanley were there, and endured one another for the sake of the company; everyone chatted together and walked briskly, skirts whipping in the cold wind; it would be good to get in again to the palace fires. They passed by where Overbury and Rochester were, nodded and received courtesies in exchange, and went on. Frances let her thoughts rove hotly over the memory of Rochester's recent embraces. He was still shy, but she would cure him. She had it clear in her mind, the accomplishment of the divorce; it could easily be sworn that Essex was impotent; she herself had been to her familiar, Mistress Anne Turner, and had obtained a drug to soak the sheets and another to give the unwelcome young husband in his drink. She could recall Essex' anguished voice, newly returned to her as he was after years abroad.

"Frankey, it *will not be.*" And he had tried again in their drugged bed, but without success, reasonably enough; besides the drugs she'd plugged herself with wool, to be sure of the matter. There was no reason for a young woman to accept a husband she would as soon not have, while Robin, Robin, was after all her own. Frances smiled to herself. Matters would point her way, by the end. It was all very well for that faggot of an Overbury to attempt to govern Robin; she'd break the friendship with her own alluring flesh. Young men were for young women, and Robin was for her. They'd go far together, let everyone watch and see. It was enough to make one almost laugh aloud, seeing the two of them standing there with her uncle Northampton close by; he disliked Overbury and all she herself had said to him had not made for the greater liking. But when Northampton came to her and murmured of what he had overheard, Frances slid from her own dislike to hatred, cold like a snake's venom. It was bad enough having Venetia Stanley, that young chit, taking Robin's eye in passing, but to say that she, Frances Howard, was unfit to be a wife, and Robin so easily led!

She would have her revenge. She would have it in a certain way. She knew already, pointedly, what she planned to do. The beautiful cold eyes regarded Northampton still standing in the garden. He'd ask the King for some impossible task for Overbury, then when there was displeasure Overbury should be taken to the Tower, and then—

Robert Carr, Viscount Rochester, was looking back not at Frances but at Venetia. He was astonished at the quick lust so young a girl aroused in him; he had never felt so for any woman, not even Frances herself. And so trammelled was he now in Frances' plots and her uncle's, both being Howards and powerful at Court, that Carr knew he had not the wit to get himself out; and Tom, who always advised him for his good, was against the marriage.

He started in a protective way to talk of Venetia when they had all gone by. "Truth to tell I covet her," he said, "and so young." One would not, of course, think of marriage; but a trifle of pleasure, before matters took their course, would be diverting, to say the least.

Overbury laughed. "She is an enchanting child," he said, "and is in love with a young man who is at present in Spain, Kenelm Digby. As his father's son I know him to be young enough; but she swears she will have none other, and awaits his return—he is studying at Salamanca—with impatience. I do not know what his mother thinks of it. Sackville is taken with her, but despite all that they say I do not think he has won her."

So Kenelm Digby's was the name to remember. Rochester's slow mind fastened on the fact. He did not know precisely how, yet, he would accomplish his will; but he meant to have Venetia, and his desire was only inflamed by the difficulty of it and by the mention of Sackville. If he himself might make use of her love's name, all might be well, and afterwards his fortunes might take him soaring where they would. It was no more than a teasing matter that occupied one's mind for the time. Once he, Rochester, was surfeited, there would be no further anxiety.

Venetia had a woman about her called Mistress Islip, who had been with her since the days in Shropshire. Out of habit Venetia called her governess, though by now she was mainly a chaperone, and lax at that. But the girl trusted her. As, day after day, Sackville and others called, Islip began to speak favourably of Rochester; how handsome he was, how generous! (He had in private been very generous to Islip.) When there was a gentleman like that how could she think of anyone else, let alone young Kenelm Digby, who was never here! "And he hath no fortune since his father was hanged as a traitor."

"His father was no more than a true friend to Catesby, who deceived him."

The colour had heightened in Venetia's

cheeks a little; she did not reply further about Kenelm; it was certainly strange that she still thought of him, but she did. As regarded Rochester, she had taken a dislike to him; the King's minion, and spoken of together with Frances Essex, whose divorce was now made final! He need not come here again. She said as much to Islip, who looked at her out of the corners of her eyes and said nothing.

A day or two later, Islip came in with a joyful countenance. Did Venetia know that Kenelm had come home, and wanted to see her privately? Her hand brushed Venetia's sleeve in a familiar, caressing gesture which made the girl uncomfortable, but she was so delighted with the message from Kenelm that she said nothing except: "Where is he? When can I see him? Will his mother let him come here?" Mary Digby, she knew, ruled her son still. But how glorious to have him home, fresh come from Spain!

"I do not know about his mother, but he asks you to meet him in the park, alone, at sunset. I think maybe you should not go; it is not a safe place," said Islip, who knew very well what was to happen. But Robin Carr had plenty of money.

"Of course I will go!"

"Not alone, surely?" She knew how to draw out her young mistress; Venetia's mild eyes flashed fire. "Of course I will go alone," she said. "We have been parted long enough and our affairs meddled with. No one shall come with me. I will take the coach."

"It would be better to hire a coach, so that you are not known."

"Very well, then, see to it."

Islip went away smiling; how easily it had all come about! That evening a plain coach came to the door, drawn by very good horses. Venetia, in a dark cloak, got in. Islip stood at the door for a moment to watch her mistress depart, her hand on the lintel: then she went in and closed the door.

The coach drove on towards the park, and already the evening was drawing in. Venetia began to be excited; it was so long since she had seen Kenelm, and nothing heard from him! A trifle of conscience gnawed at her; she had not had time to answer a letter of his that had reached her, so busied was she with the frivolous doings at Court. But after tonight there would be no need to reproach oneself. Would he have grown much? He must be enormous, and by now very learned.

The sun was setting and the shadows grew longer. There were few about, but suddenly a party of five or six men set about the coach, which slowed and stopped. "Drive on," said a voice. The man jerked the coach door open and came in, with another. They were none that she knew. To her consternation, the leader drew out a poniard. "Say but a word, or scream," he said, "and this"—he thrust it toward her—"goes into your throat, my pretty. If you are quiet there will be no trouble." He motioned impatiently, and the coachman, whose face she had not seen, obeyed. Three men had entered the coach and drawn the curtains. Venetia was filled with such terror she could not even speak; who were these men, and where was she being taken?

It was a long journey; it continued through the night. She had tried to guess which way they went, but no longer knew where she could be, and she was very much afraid. What did they want with her? It could not be riches. She had heard of other abductions; of heiresses, or else of great beauties who had inflamed men's hearts so that they forced them into marriage. Venetia knew that she was beautiful and that many, like Ned Sackville, desired her openly, but without marriage. Was the coach Sackville's, and were they going to Dorset? She did not know, and would not ask the men, some of whom sat silent by her, while the rest rode with the horses. One sat at each side of her, another opposite. One of them started to light and smoke a pipe of tobacco, which disgusted her. She was too much afraid to bid him put it out. When it grew dark, the coachman stopped and lit the lanterns, then drove on while the horsemen departed. She was very tired, the first fright having subsided and leaving, instead, a great weariness. She must not break down and cry in front of these men. She closed her eyes and tried to sleep, but could not. The lit coach trundled on through the dark.

Had she slept after all? The coach had

drawn up with a jolt at last and the men muttered together, then thankfully took themselves off. The dawn was breaking and through the grey light Venetia could see the front of a great house, with lawns about it, and an old woman standing ready at the door, smiling at her. She was thankful to see anyone of the kind. She loosened the catch of the door and stumbled out. "Please tell me where they have brought me," she said with such dignity as she could muster, flushed and tousled as she knew she must be after the long journey. The old woman gave a bob and said: "Never trouble yourself, my lady; you are with friends. Come inside; there is a good bed waiting."

But whose bed? Venetia thought; it was evident they would not tell her, and she mounted the stairs with the old woman carrying a candle in front of her. She was almost asleep on her feet, and when the bed was reached saw only that it was private, hung with rich curtains, and seemed comfortable, with clean linen laid. She let the woman help unlace her, then fell into the bed and slept at once.

She awoke to hear someone moving

about the room. She cried out and heard him—it was a man—say: "Do not be afraid. I am going to light a candle." She saw the tinder spark, and in that instant saw, shadowy but known, the face of Rochester. So he was the author of all this! He should not have her! He should not!

"Leave me," she said, as the candlelight flared to reveal his face again, the pretty boy's face with the short, pointed fair beard. He held the candle above her, smiling; he looked, Venetia decided, like a devil. She stared up at him for instants; what was she to do? If she got up out of the bed it would reveal her undress, and if she stayed—But he spoke again, gently enough, using the charm that had charmed the King.

"Forgive me. I will do everything you wish. Believe that it was for love of you that I had to do this thing. I will be your servant in all ways. But do not deny me, I beg, beautiful Venetia! I have never loved any woman as I love you."

But you are going to marry Frances Essex, she thought; the banns were called. What sort of a simpleton did he think her? It was perhaps because Dad had left her alone in London with Mistress Islip, so that any man might grow familiar with her if he chose. Well, she would look after herself. "Then if you are my servant, leave me now," she said calmly. "That is my first order."

He looked at her beautiful face and tangled bright hair on the pillows; even now she had the child's innocence that had attracted him. A kind of shame came to Carr; he would have to win her by gentleness. "I will leave you, then," he said. "In the meantime, regard this house and everything in it as yours. Permit me to have your company, nothing more. I swear I will make you love me, and nothing shall be done without love between us."

Then nothing shall be done, she heard herself thinking. Robin Carr was himself simple after all. "Go now," she said, "and I will tidy myself." He went, and presently the old woman came in with a tray of food. It was delicious and daintily served, and Venetia found that she was hungry. Carr came in again and waited on her, eating nothing himself. Afterwards he said: "I will show you the garden," and she let him lead her there in the by now bright daylight. She looked about for ways of escape; for escape she must, if possible without anyone's knowing that she had been taken away. No young woman's reputation would survive such a story.

The gardens were extensive and well-kept. Rochester showed her the ponds, the maze —she did not permit him to take her into it—the brilliant flower-beds where all manner of flowers bloomed, some from as far away as Persia; the roses were particularly fine. Rochester picked a striped rose and gave it to her; they walked so, her hand laid lightly on his arm, her other holding the rose on its long stalk. "Do you know roses, sweetheart?" she heard him ask. His hot blue eyes burned her, and she withdrew her hand.

"Do not call me that, for it is not so," she told him. Rochester sighed, with a trifle of impatience; he was not accustomed to wait as long for his will. He murmured an apology, took Venetia's hand again, and guided her across the lawns, talking the while of plants and their growing. At Ferniehurst in Scotland, where he had come from, his mother had had a herb-garden. He had been a younger son and had ridden to England to seek his fortune, and had found it. "I love Sherborne greatly," he said, then almost bit his tongue; he should not have let her know where she was, where the long ride in darkness had brought her.

Sherborne. She knew the name. This was the house that had been the home of Sir Walter Raleigh, who now lay in the Tower. Raleigh's wife had gone down on her knees to beg the King to let her keep it, the beloved place; but James had only replied: "Na, na; I maun ha'e it for Carr." And Carr had taken possession of it, and soon would bring his bride here. Venetia smiled to hide her thoughts; she must escape. She had been watching carefully as they walked through the gardens, and she thought she had the glimmering of a plan. Her bedroom window looked out on the place they were now passing; there was a little eminence with an arbour on it, garlanded with some creeping plant with foam-like blossoms. Beyond it was the wall. If she could she would gain the arbour tonight; but she must not let him come to her, she must not; she must leave here. The countryside was unknown: she could not be certain where she was, except that, as she had lately learned, this house was Sherborne. But anything was better than to stay and let Robert Carr take her as his whore. She dropped her eyelids, and spoke in her gentle voice.

"I believe I am tired. The journey yesterday was very long. I would like to go to my chamber. There is a dew falling, do you not feel it?"

She made pretence to shiver in the sunshine, and he was all concern. He accompanied her to the stairs, and watched as she ascended to her room; he was still enchanted with her, still thought in his fool's mind only of the satisfaction of his immediate desire. With the power he had, he could claim anything; but he regretted letting Venetia know the name of the place. Yet she was secure; he would have her by the end, but it had best not be long. Frances was a demanding mistress, and would note his absence and write, or send a messenger, soon.

The old woman was still about the room, and when Venetia demanded that she unlace her came accordingly, and made the girl ready for going to bed. The linen was again fresh. Venetia made herself lie down and close her eyes, and at last felt evening come; soon, soon let it be night! For the first time she began to be afraid of the coming journey; she knew no one here-abouts, and all manner of things could happen. But anything was better than to let Carr have his way, as though she had been a milkmaid. She felt resolution grown strong in her, and thought soon of Kenelm. Were he to know of this he would fell Robert Carr with his fist.

"Dear Kenelm," she murmured, and soon slept.

She awoke to hear the old woman, in a room nearby, snoring. It was bright moon-light. Venetia slipped out of bed, quietly and quickly dressed herself, then took a sheet from the bed, then another. She tied them together and went to the window. It was not so far to the ground.

She opened, carefully, the casement that it might not creak; tied the upper sheet to the bar, then let herself out of the window, sliding down the support she had made; it held. Quickly, in the moonlight, she found her way across the garden, moving in shadow. The arbour was there. She stood behind it for a moment, panting; then climbed the wall. This part was dangerous; if he were to look out of a window, he would see her clearly against the light of the moon. The wall was too high. She slid down again, found her garters, and tied them together to form a support; it was not so far down as the window had been; after all, she was safe. Cropped grass confronted her, grey in the moonlight. She began to run, walk, run again, holding up her skirts: she must not twist her ankle as she went. Every moment took her further from Carr. There was a paling now, to keep the deer out; she could climb it easily enough, but took leisure not to spike herself, and landed at last on rougher ground, with trees nearby. At first she was glad of the trees, as she could no longer be seen in their shadow; then she began to be afraid. Where had she come to? Which way should she go? The only way was, of course, to make the distance from Carr ever further, and Venetia hurried ahead as she could, often stopped by thrusting branches, often surprised by hollows in the ground. The moon rose high. Had he discovered yet that she had gone? But he must not, could not, find her now; she knew a moment's triumph. Wherever the forest led her, there she must go; someone, somewhere, would be found to help her.

It took longer than she thought. She knew the moon went down and morning began to be grey at last, a streak on the horizon; the sun rose in the east, she must be going that way, or was it leading her back to Sherborne? She came to the knowledge that she was completely lost, and already very tired; her shoes were muddy with the forest ways and she had torn her cloak on brambles. She gathered it about her, looked round, saw nothing, heard nothing except the scurry of some small animal in the leaves. Everything was quiet, and she could go no further. She lay down in a mossy place, wrapped her cloak about her, and tried to sleep; but it was very cold, there was no warmth in the moon. Venetia began to cry. The tears coursed down her cheeks and soaked her bodice beneath the cloak; and her sobbing could be heard, clear and soft in the night. Soon, surely, it would be morning; by then some new plan would have come to her, surely, surely; she could not die here in the forest. If only Kenelm were here, to put his strong arms round her and warm and comfort her! But he was far away.

The presence of danger remained to be dealt with; she heard a heavier, padding sound that the birds and awakening animals could not possibly make, and turning sharply saw a great grey mask with slavering jaws. It was a wolf, and it had sighted her. Venetia screamed aloud. If even Rochester would come! But the wolf was hungry. It sniffed round about, as if to make sure of her, and she tried to escape; it nosed her gown, and she tried to fend it off, and it fastened its teeth in her. She screamed again, with blood coming swiftly, though the pain itself was frozen with fear; having smelt blood the beast was the more eager. It began to drag at her, to take her away for its meal; she screamed again and again, certain now that she would leave her bones in a wolf's den; how could it have happened? But it was true; and then by a miracle, there were other sounds, even as she smelt the animal's foetid breath and saw its yellowed fangs, opened ready to devour her.

A huntsman had come. His clothing was of leather, brown against the leaves. There were dogs, welcome baying hounds, behind him. They must have been after a stag, but they scented the wolf and closed in, and the poor beast fled and was soon torn to pieces.

"Here! Here! Help me, oh, help me!" Supposing he had not seen her? But he had a face she surely knew. He slid from the saddle and came to her. He was not Ned Sackville, of the large hands and feet, but he looked like him in feature, none more so. This was Dorset himself, who had nigh ruined himself with venery.

The Earl of Dorset knelt by the girl; she had fainted, and no wonder. He called his servants, suddenly aware that, having been out after a stag all night, he needed to shave. This was a most fair lady, even with blood on her white arm. Dorset held her close till she recovered, then said softly: "You are safe. When you have rested I will take you home." Where was her home? Her clothes were those of a lady. "The wolf is dead," he said. "How fortunate that I was nearby!"

"Home," he heard her reply wearily; where was that? Suddenly she heard herself pouring out all her trouble, glad to have found a willing listener who did not covet her for her body; or did he, was he like all men? He was looking at her, she saw, in a particular way, and she made herself sit up out of his embrace.

"You are safe," he said again. "I am the Earl of Dorset. And you, most fair and unfortunate one, who are you and how came you here?"

Dorset, she thought. Sackville's brother, and no better than Sackville, not a doubt. She had escaped two dangers only to fall into a third. She drew herself up and remembered that she was a Stanley. They were surrounded by the forest, only now beginning to glimmer with dawn; through it, Venetia thought she began to see stone towers. If only she had gone that way earlier!

"Whose house is that?" she asked. Dorset did not take his gaze from her face, and replied: "Dame Horsey's. But I will not take you to her; she is a tiresome old dame, and a Papist."

He must have mistaken her for a village girl, Venetia thought. She made herself smile. "Dame Horsey of Nether Compton?" There was some kinship, if she could remember what it was. "Will you please take me there?"

His glance faltered. So it was good blood, the blood that still leaked from her forearm. One could not take advantage of a young lady in such a state. It would be best in any case to get the wound dressed, but he himself wasn't going to cross the path of that old Papist bitch again. Yet he did not regret losing the stag's scent and finding this delightful young lady.

"We must meet again," he said. "I regret that I cannot take you myself to Nether Compton, I have some quarrel with its mistress, none of my seeking." He had in fact made certain improper overtures to meek-seeming little Sibyl, old madam's granddaughter; that had been a mistake. "My servants shall conduct you," he promised amiably.

Venetia let herself be conducted, almost fainting again on the pommel of a servant's horse. She was uncertain whether or not Dame Horsey would know who she was, but it might serve for the time. She would send word to Dad as soon as she might, and he must send money; after that she would be able to fend for herself, but just now could not.

3

VENETIA remembered very little more until she found herself in a comfortable bed in a room with a fire freshly blazing, and a benevolent-seeming dowager seated by the window-sill. Venetia opened her eyes, blinked, and smiled.

"So you are awake, child," said Dame Horsey. "I trust you are recovering." The sharp eyes dwelt on Venetia's arm, which was covered with a dressing containing herbal ointment. "That plaster will ensure, I trust, that it heals without leaving a scar. A most unpleasant experience for you; it is a mercy you were within call of help."

She rose and advanced with all the majesty of stiff satins and a farthingale. Her cap was of lawn, and a neatly laundered ruff set off her grey hair, combed high on a frame. She wore no rings, but gave the impression of being a person of substance; keys jangled at her waist, as if to assure the onlooker that she would rely on the services of no housekeeper except herself.

"And now, my child," she said kindly enough, "who are you? It is unusual, to say the least, for so young a girl as yourself to be alone in a forest at dawn, as they told me, without servants or other aid. Where are your kin, and how came you here?"

Venetia saw that it was useless to tell anything but the truth; this old woman would not be deceived. In any case, she had nothing with which to blame herself. She told Dame Horsey how she had been abducted from London and brought to Sherborne, and the details of her escape. The old dame nodded briefly.

"You have behaved with courage," she said, "but it is a pity that you spent a night under his roof. He hath no good name hereabouts. The fewer persons who know of all that the better. I shall honour your confidence." She nodded again, briskly. "Now, have you any friends in circumstances that may bear out your story? I myself believe you, but my granddaughter lives with me, and I must be sure she does not meet uncertain company. I am putting matters plainly, as you will understand, I hope."

Venetia's colour rose. It was difficult to oblige so particular a lady; in fact it was some time since she herself had seen anyone except Islip and her own assiduous gentlemen visitors. She sought desperately in her mind for someone of whom this old lady would approve, and remembered Kenelm's mother. Surely Lady Digby would understand the need to mention her name? "Although I recall," Venetia reminded herself, "that she did not like me."

"I knew Lady Digby slightly at Gothurst; but it is a long way from here," she said. But the dowager's hands had already raised themselves in joy.

"Mary Digby!" she said. "I know her well, and knew poor Everard; and, more than that, we will soon be related by marriage, for she and I have decided that Sibyl had best marry her son Kenelm. It is a hard matter nowadays to bestow a proper dowry in the right quarter without having it squandered by some rascal; manners and morals are not what they used to be." She talked on, while Venetia grew pale and grief-stricken. Kenelm to marry! Of course it was to be expected. And she herself had no dowry to speak of. This old woman's granddaughter—one would certainly dislike her—was fortunate. She made herself murmur a few words in order not to seem strange: but the relentless voice went on.

"You must stay here, at any rate, till you are recovered; not many can boast of a wolf-bite and live. You will see your friends shortly; young Kenelm Digby is returned from Spain, and he and his mother will in fact be here the day after tomorrow. How singular that you should have arrived just at this time!"

After she had gone, Venetia turned and wept into her pillows. The gods had made her the butt of fortune. Now for the first time she realized how greatly she had relied on Kenelm, as well as remembering that he loved her. All men were fickle; but at least she would see him when he came here for his betrothal.

Dame Horsey's grandchild was a meek young woman with china-blue eyes and hair combed back smoothly. Nothing she did was other than seemly, and as she had herself foreseen Venetia disliked her at sight. She had found in any case that it took longer than might have been expected to feel quite herself again, took one or two turns in the garden and then went back to bed; the wound had healed to a scar before she came hesitantly downstairs at last. By then Mary Digby was seated in the hall, and a huge young man by her, talking with Sibyl. Venetia paused on the stairs, and Kenelm looked up. How greatly grown he was! And he, on beholding her—

"Venetia!" The name burst from him, and he hurried at once towards the staircase. She felt her hand taken firmly in his huge paw, and was led forwards; Lady Digby and her hostess were already disturbed, but Sibyl looked exactly the same as usual; no doubt she was without strong feelings of any kind. Venetia gazed at Kenelm, then realized she must after all be polite to her hostess; she made a curtsey, and a second to Kenelm's mother. The latter had aged and there was much grey in her hair. Kenelm's own curled as it had always done. How greatly she longed to talk to him, to hear about Spain, about himself, and if he still loved her! But perhaps he was trapped by this unwelcome marriage. The dowry was everything: she must not keep him from it. She disengaged her hand and he let it go.

"Come to the fire, my dear," said Dame Horsey. "This child was savaged by a wolf, and very fortunately it happened nearby us. She says you know her." The voice was emphatic, and Kenelm's mother made a nod, but said no more than that.

Later that evening Venetia found a note in her glove. It was from Kenelm. *Come with the hunt tomorrow*, it read. *We will part from it and meet when we can.*

It was not too easy for her to mount a horse yet, but she did it; and all about were the sounds she had been used to hear in Shropshire, of hounds baying and the impatient neighing and trampling of horses; her own that they had given her was a nervous beast and she hoped that she could hold him. She saw Kenelm mounted in his turn, and kept near; and the hunt made off. Venetia galloped with it a little way into the remembered forest, and something of her earlier dread returned; if she should miss Kenelm after all, and lose herself again! But she could only turn away, when she could, from the main party, and let her horse lose her among the trees. These closed in, with hardly a path left to walk on; and Venetia slowed the mount and let it dawdle, then heard a cheerful hail.

"Venetia!"

He was here; he had done as she had and as he had promised, and had lost the following; they were together after so long. For the first time they embraced as man and woman, then tied their horses' reins to a branch, and sat themselves down, gazing on one another. It was Eden here, no longer the dreaded forest; he was with her again, as it had used to be in their childhood; but so differently! How large he was! How she loved him, and admired his deep rich voice, telling her not of the swarm of black-clad students in Salamanca but of his love for her, and how it had never faltered despite all the Spanish beauties in the world!

"And I wrote to you, but you did not answer, cruel one." He looked at her, seated contentedly by him; her cheeks were still the colour of the damask rose, and presently Kenelm made a gesture he could not help, and Venetia sprang back from him, tears in her eyes.

"You are the same as all the rest. Begone from me; I am not your whore." The tears rained down her cheeks suddenly and he took her in his arms and kissed them away. "Have no fear," he said when he could. "I love you too greatly to hurt you, my queen. Have no fear."

Their tongues touched; they sat there closely together while the hours passed, and when evening fell took the saddle again, but found they had lost themselves indeed. It was fortunate that at last they met a woodsman of Dame Horsey's, who told them the way home; and when they got there, neither the old dame nor Mary Digby was pleased. To be lost for half a day, in a wood with Venetia Stanley! Mary by now had told their hostess precisely what a designing little minx the girl was, and Dame Horsey began to be sorry she had ever entertained her, wolf or no wolf. As for Sibyl, she sat and sewed a seam. Nobody troubled her, then or later.

"You dare to speak to me of your love for that wanton? You know nothing of the matter; how can you, at your age? I loved your father as well as any wife may love a man, and I never saw him till the day of our betrothal; it was arranged sensibly by our parents. Because I am a poor widow woman you will not obey me in such ways, or in any way."

His large body blocked the light from the window: she heard his deep voice replying calmly, thoughtfully; it was impossible to make him angry. "You will not speak of Venetia as a wanton again," he told her, and from her heart she cried out to him, but he would not heed her; she reminded herself that after all he had been to Spain, had gone to the university there, was no longer a child. Yet it was as a child he answered her, with a child's innocence.

"I cannot make the marriage you would have for me," he said. "I have loved Venetia, as I told you, from the time that I could first think. I could not make a wife of any other."

"She is too flighty for a wife," said Mary angrily. She rose and began to turn about the room. "What good Dame Horsey thinks of us I cannot tell; she hath every right to be displeased. It would have been a fortunate marriage for you, situated as you are with little enough money after your father's arraignment, and few nowadays will wed with a Papist for the trouble and the fines. I had made all ready, and now you have spoilt it." Her face began to pout with the lines deepening on it, and of a sudden Kenelm swooped and kissed her. The warmth of the kiss reminded Mary of her husband and she gave way to tears.

"If only your father had been here," she moaned. He smiled down at her.

"Well might I wish it, and yet he is not, and I must fend for us both. Do not be angry, my mother, if I do not marry yet. Let me travel a little, and I will prove to you that my love for Venetia is stronger than time and place. Meantime, I greatly desire to see the places where other men live, and where wisdom is, and knowledge." He spread his hands and looked down at them. Then he faced her again; his little harried mother, growing old and fretful with the hardness of her days. "Madam, you live as you will, lacking my father," he told her.

"Let me do likewise, at least for the time."

"You should be breeding heirs for your father's name, and here you are ready to go off abroad again, as soon as I had got you home, and the marriage—"

"Forget the marriage," he said lightly. "I doubt me Dame Horsey hath repented by now of her bargain in me. Leave it at present, my mother; in time it will be seen, in time, in time."

"You must spend some time at Oxford: your father would have wished it."

"I will obey. But afterwards—"

"Afterwards," said Mary Digby, "we will see."

He saw Venetia by arrangement in London before he left for France. He took a ring from his finger that had belonged to his father; it was a great diamond, long hidden by Mary Digby from the sheriffs and the searchers, and lately given to him now he was of an age. His mother would know nothing of the gift; he would go straight abroad. The ring fitted Venetia's narrow finger; he slid it on.

"That is to prove my love, and that I am ever faithful," he told her. "If you ever doubt me, look at that stone's brightness and believe me true."

The easy tears rose in her eyes and she went to where there were scissors, and before him cut off a lock of her long curling hair and gave it to him. Its brightness shone in the clear light from the window. He kissed it, then took off his coat and pushed up his shirt sleeve, and wound the lock carefully about his arm.

"I shall wear it always," he swore. Then he took her in his great strong arms and kissed her. "Do you be true to me, my love, and one day we will be one."

She was still tearful. "I doubt that day will ever come; your mother likes me not."

He smiled, the smile spreading over his face like a sunbeam. "But I," he said, "love you greatly."

So he rode off, and she returned dismally to Islip, whom she had meant to have dismissed, but somehow it had not happened, there had been such business since she came back from the country and had to have her own things about her, and nobody else knew where to find them, and Islip and she had said nothing of what had occurred, and there it was; and Kenelm riding off, just when she had been full of joy at sight of him. How was she to go on, neither wife nor widow? But in his great comforting presence everything of that kind seemed to melt, only returning to itself again after he had gone away. She did not know when, if ever, she would see him again, but he had promised to write, and she would wait for that. She kept herself meantime close in her rooms, and only heard such tattle about the Court as Islip brought her, and did not receive any of the gentlemen who came, and of them only Ned Sackville persisted, and when she denied him her presence sent her flowers.

Kenelm endured the dreaming spires for as long as he might; one thing that kept him there, among the assembly of noble small boys often whipped and lectured, was the memory of his great-grandfather, who had hallooed with his horn and disturbed the quiet colleges in the small hours; also, there was, at Gloucester College, Deacon Laud. He was a small intent man with bright eyes who darted about on his own business and supervised the students under his care as well; Kenelm had many arguments with him concerning the Church of England. He himself, as a Papist, could expect no promotion in England to any profession, and indeed he felt drawn to none.

"Why should we, an island people, be subject to a foreign potentate such as the Pope is? Why should the King have to fear excommunication when he is our Church's Head?" Laud's little hands fluttered and his lawn sleeves billowed in the breeze that blew along the sleeping Isis. Kenelm did not venture to answer him, but as always admired his industry and his respect for great language. "We have in the new Bible the noblest of phrasing. Let it put paid to the interpretations of other men that shall dismay us. I speak not only of the Papists but of the new so-called brethren that assemble in their own places and hold meetings without God's law."

Kenelm had little knowledge of the newcome Puritans as yet. He surveyed Laud closely and wondered if it would be tactful to remind him that the Pope had offered him a cardinal's hat should he agree to adhere to the Church of Rome.

"Surely," said Kenelm, "it were meet to be at one with the whole word besides ourselves."

"Look at what the world hath done in conquering Bohemia, and in laying waste the King's daughter's husband's Palatinate. She hath nowhere to lay her head."

But politics should not enter into it. Kenelm continued with his own devotions, aided by several other Catholic students who had been sent of necessity to Gloucester Hall. He made few friends besides Laud and Allen but would remember the former for the rest of his life, in especial after the determined Archbishop of Canterbury, as Laud was by then, had been thrown into prison and at last beheaded by the Puritans for his steadfastness in belief.

Tom Allen was a mathematician, and Kenelm would visit him and experiment with his astrolabe and compasses, and hear his talk. Tom was one of the few people with whom the young man felt at home in Oxford; the curriculum was narrow and defeated any enterprise or enquiry. Yet once he had heard Tom's voice speaking of the symmetry of the parabola or the squares of numbers, or logarithms, then would take heart; and there were personal stories as well, as for instance when Tom had been staying at some house and the maids, making his bed, had heard a ticking noise under the pillow, had thought the object lying there was his familiar and had thrown it out into the moat. "But it caught on a branch of an elder," said Tom, "and I got my watch back safely; but they thought me the more of a wizard for doing so, no doubt."

The Court was diverted, perhaps even titillated, by the trial for murder of the new Earl and Countess of Somerset. The truth about Overbury's death had come out by way of an apothecary's boy encountered in Flushing. The dead man had been slowly poisoned over the months, being sent gifts by the Countess to beguile his imprisonment; little cakes and tarts and jellies, arriving regularly. Still Overbury did not die, although the uneaten jellies turned green; in the end, when he was skin and bone, they gave him a mercury enema, which killed him. Lesser folk than the

Somersets were questioned, and Frances' familiar Anne Turner hanged at last; as for the King, he slobbered over Somerset and kissed him many times going down Whitehall staircase, saying he could not live without his Robin; then when the man had ridden off said: "And now, by God, I will never look on your face again."

The pair were arraigned; Frances went to her trial wearing a black dress with lawn at the throat and wrists. The details of her divorce from Essex were made public: *to make strait portals where wide gates had been.* Later the King commuted the death-sentence to imprisonment in the Tower for husband and wife. In after years it was said of Frances Somerset that she harboured a growth within her which prevented intercourse. Perhaps the gods took their revenge in this way. After some years the pair were released, but never came again to Court. In the place of Robin Carr now was young George Villiers, a long-legged youth the King swore looked like St. Stephen. In time he would be ennobled, as Somerset had been, but would rise to dizzier heights in his day. The world knew him as Buckingham, free with his favours, shining with jewels and feathered plumes; abducting an heiress who was accordingly forced to marry him, and spending her dowry on his pleasure. But the King could see no wrong in him and Prince Charles, now Prince of Wales, first loathed and then adored "Steenie".

The Queen died in 1619. She never knew that her daughter Elizabeth, whose marriage she had so deplored, would have her fate settled in Bohemia by the Battle of the White Mountain, at which her husband was not even present to fight. Elizabeth had urged Frederick to accept the crown of Bohemia, and paid for it the rest of her life, as a pensioner in Holland. She bore eleven children before the Palsgrave died, of a stupid cold caught in Sweden; and at The Hague became a lure to visiting nobility and a legend to Europe, the Protestant Winter Queen.

Kenelm at last rode the Dover Road again, thankful to be free, two servants riding behind him with the baggage. There was a trifle of rain but it did not trouble him; he turned up the collar of his heavy cloak and cantered on. The ship awaiting him was no royal vessel this time, but the ordinary packet; yet it would take him to unimagined places, to seaports, fortresses, France, France. His heart sang within him and he felt the soft warm strength of Venetia's hair wound about his flesh, his talisman. He would never part with it while he lived, he promised himself; they had one another's vows, and one day he would ride back, but till then, there was the world to see!

The packet set sail uneventfully, the rain spattering on the sea and pitting it into a thousand rebellious droplets while Kenelm watched from the deck. As before, he could not endure the closeness of a cabin; the Channel itself was part of his adventure. So small a space, and yet it divided folk as different as monkeys from parrots; and the language, this time, he could speak. He let the rain and spray soak his hair, and wiped the running wet from his face with his sleeve, till he could see Calais at last, towers rearing out of the mist the rain made; old Calais, that had once belonged to England.

Sackville brought certain news to Venetia

from Court; Sir Thomas Overbury was dead in the Tower. Everyone knew he had been sent there in April, under the King's displeasure for some matter connected with refusing an embassy. He was young to die; had it been a fever? At any rate it was forgotten that autumn by everyone of note except Overbury's parents; Court was preparing for the Somerset wedding. "One had only just grown used to calling Robin Carr Rochester, and now he is made an earl," drawled Ned Sackville, eyeing Venetia where she sat with the September sunshine making a glory of her hair; the cut lock had grown into a little tendril, which hung by her cheeks. "What will you wear to the wedding, my dear?" asked Islip, who was with them. Whatever embarrassment anyone felt at again meeting with Robin Carr had been overcome; such happenings were the way of the world, and the new Earl's blue eyes had met those of Venetia once, with a careful lack of expression, after her return to Whitehall, when they met at a card-game. Venetia had played her cards calmly and had won, which pleased her. It was not likely that Somerset, to give him his new title, would trouble her again; he was dominated by his bride-to-be, whose kin had got him the title from James. The divorced countess would keep her rank, with no bones broken. The wedding day dawned at last and the Court noted ironically that Frances, proceeding down the aisle on the arm of her Uncle Northampton, wore her golden hair combed loose about her shoulders in token of her virginity, and Somerset himself did not seem to be mourning his erstwhile friend's death. The pair returned from the altar handsome and loving together, and before the feasting and dancing afterwards an ode was read which a Court poet had written for the occasion. Venetia wondered how soon the Earl of Somerset would take his bride to Sherborne, to show her the house, the garden, and the arbour on the little hill.

"Call him King of France? Whipped every morning for the sins of the day before, he was, when the old lady had him in her charge all his boyhood. Was that the way to make a man of him like his father? Ah, those were the good days, the days of

Henri IV. Wanted every peasant to have a chicken in his pot on Sundays, he did. He would have managed it but for that madman Ravaillac and his murdering knife. Well, we tore *him* to bits; but it didn't give us back our good king again. Yet at least young Louis is ruling now in his own right, which means the Duc de Luynes tells him what to do, and the old lady herself has trundled off to Angers, which place is welcome to her, great fat spendthrift of an Italian bitch that she is, and mean as well, they say. King Henri should have stuck to his first wife and not married out of France. *La Reine Margot* was a high-stepper, if you like. There might have been a son in time, if they'd tried hard enough and King Henri had spent less time with his women and more with his wife. The *Vert Galant* they used to call him. I can remember his riding past here in the old coach that had belonged to the Valois, with a pretty demoiselle beside him, but poor enough horses; he tried to save money in such ways and spend it on the country. A great hook nose he had, and they say stank like a brock; but since Saint Louis there has never been anyone in France who was kinder to ordinary folk. A father to his people, Henri IV was; and now he's gone, whether to purgatory or not God knows, for despite everything they say he was always a Huguenot at heart. Many pray for his soul still, even after ten years."

"So there is not much life now in Paris," Kenelm said, and sipped the thin wine. It was a run-down tavern near the Queen Dowager's avenue of planted chestnut trees, that they said was the only good thing she had ever done for France. Kenelm had seen the mean narrow ways of the walled capital of France, the new palace of the Louvre with its creamy stone, where the sombre young Louis XIII lived with his advisers and his young Spanish wife, with whom he did not get on; it was whispered that Anne of Austria had got herself a miscarriage romping with her ladies-in-waiting, and the King was displeased with her. Kenelm had himself seen the famed beauty of Anne but had not been set on fire; in the act of kissing her white hands, he had remembered Venetia, also the Queen's dull brother whom he had met in Madrid. He would not stay in Paris, where even the Sorbonne was closed at this season: he would go, instead, out of curiosity to see the fat Italian widow of Henri IV at Angers and see what entertainment she could provide; then he might well make for Italy.

He tossed the loquacious innkeeper a coin and left the tavern, walking quickly down the broad way between the chestnut plantings they were already beginning to call the *Cours la Reine*, and plunging into the city. A few dejected, poorly clad citizens stood about in the black mud and jumbled buildings and high roofs, staring. Nothing seemed to have changed in Paris since good King Henri had been done to death almost ten years ago.

They stared at Kenelm as he went past them, the people: the huge healthy curly-headed young man might have been somebody out of a fable, removed from their daily grind and toil for bread. With his cloak of plain wool—he never dressed grandly—and his hair free under his high hat, he had the happy look about him of someone who loves life for itself, shouldering his way through the alleys. The days were gone when such men had chosen to live in Paris. Now, everything was down-at-heel and there were few rich visitors: and not enough work and not enough money. They watched him pass by, and then forgot him, as one forgets dreams.

He had taken the advice of Mélanie de Chevreuse, a kinswoman by marriage of that duchess who had lately romped with Anne of Austria at the Louvre and caused a royal disaster. The duchess was not, therefore, in favour at the moment and Kenelm did not meet her; but Madame Mélanie advised him about many things in Paris. She was about forty years old, wise, and could be mischievous, and he listened to what she had to say about the rebel Court of the Queen Mother, Marie de Médicis, at Angers.

"Go there," said Mélanie. "In Paris it is dull and all the colleges are shut. I myself am making for Angers, but do you ride more slowly through the heart of France towards it; it is safe enough now that *she* is no longer confined by her son at Blois, whence she escaped."

The sallow face crinkled suddenly with

mirth. "She was too fat to climb down the rope ladder, so two noblemen carried her in a wrapped cloak, like a sack, and she reached the ground thus and some vineyards, and hid herself there somehow till help came. She holds a pleasant Court at Angers, for she is constantly looking for diversion." She had stopped talking and had let her knowing eyes rest pleasurably on Kenelm.

He listened, bowed, and left her; and had indeed ridden through France's heart at his leisure, seeing the flax-fields with their lavender bloom, and haystacks ruined by rain and poor folk starving. He ate when he could and stayed at inns by the wayside, some good and others bad, and noted everything until he came within sight of Angers itself, a bustling market town where lace was sold in the streets. He bought none, but made his way in due course up to the castle, whose many great turrets of striped stone still wore their conical roofs from the days of tournaments. The moat was broad and Kenelm had to prove his identity before being permitted to enter the great yard, where guards stood about idly, their lances

131

shining in the sun. A sound of music came and soon he entered the place where they were dancing; the tune was one he knew and he whistled it to himself while at the same time watching the company, who wore masks. A fat woman sat on a throne surrounded by courtiers; she seemed sullen and there was no laughter, but the dance filled the silence, and Kenelm went to the Queen Mother with an introduction, bowed, and kissed her plump hand. He saw the round eyes brighten behind the mask.

"Ah," she said, "you are the Englishman. They are not gallant. Do you dance?"

"After my fashion, Madame." He was in fact a good dancer, light on his feet as many heavy men are. He caught the eye of Madame Mélanie, among the company, and asked her to partner him in the pavon. Her eyes twinkled as she took his arm. "Madame is much taken with you," she murmured. "I can tell, well as I know her. She is weary of life and left much to her own devices since the King was killed, and the Maréchal d'Ancre."

"I understand her husband was not faithful."

"Do not speak so loudly. He visited her much in bed. A woman who has had that experience will miss it when it is no longer hers." They were circling the floor in the slow measure. "Afterwards," she said, "stay near; there will be wine and refreshment, then more dancing, then who knows?"

Kenelm felt himself blushing. He was the only unmasked dancer in the hall: the round unsated eyes of the Queen Mother followed him wherever he went, and it occurred to him that Mélanie must have said something of him to her before he came. He began to feel embarrassed. The wine was good and the food eatable; he was hungry, and downed a good meal. Everyone about him was eating and belching, some falling to the floor after too much wine. There did not seem to be polite manners here any more than at the Court of King James. Kenelm prepared to take himself off back to his inn; but he was informed that Madame de Chevreuse wanted further speech with him.

To his astonishment, Mélanie took his

133

hand firmly in her grasp, and led him out of the great hall into another room behind a curtain, where there was a bed and, on the wall, certain hangings depicting the Apocalypse. He stared at the shivering figure of John the Divine and felt an affinity with him and then at the curtain, which parted to reveal a tall stout figure. The fat woman who was Louis XIII's mother beckoned him to the bed. She felt the muscles of his arm knowingly, and smiled, revealing strong white teeth well preserved despite her age.

"I am overcome," she said in bad French, "by so fierce a flame of desire that I long—how can I say it?—I long, young man, to be your subject, to lie in your arms."

She wore the practised smile of the harlot. Kenelm felt memory rush at him with the name of her dead lover, d'Ancre. "Madame," he heard himself say desperately, "remember that you are nevertheless a queen, and I a subject. Your dignity bids me forbear."

"Nature made us all equal: Ah, come, let us not waste time," she said, and tried to pull him down on the bed. Kenelm felt determination strengthen him; he was not going to become this fat old woman's lover. Stumbling words seemed to issue themselves from his mouth; he heard himself telling her, without naming Venetia, that his heart was already given. The Queen flushed. "You were nourished with the milk of tigers," she said, "and nursed on a rock." Her eyes had regained the sullen look they had had when he first saw her. She had not let go of his arm and he wondered how to break away with decency; then there came a noise from without, a sudden sound of shouting and clash of swords.

"*Mon Dieu!* What has happened?" cried the Queen. "It is my son, perhaps." Her face was still flushed with late fury and she seemed to care more about her person than about the source of danger, whatever it was. "I will find out for you," said Kenelm firmly, and left her there. He almost ran into a posse of soldiers, who were making their way from the outer yard which had once been a tiltyard; he had no means of knowing whether they were invaders or invaded, but fighting had started and a man lay on the ground.

Kenelm felt a kind of madness rise; at least he was free. He drew his sword and shouldered his way, when he could, down the yard to the gate and gave the guards, who had let the King's men enter, a heavy bribe.

"You must tell everyone that Kenelm Digby has been killed in the fighting," he told them, and watched his golden louis d'or change hands. The guard winked.

"Be assured, monsieur, I know very well what to say." He was not perturbed by the fighting: it must have been arranged.

"See to it, then. Do not fail me." And Kenelm made haste to leave the place, still marvelling that so much had happened since his arrival. He found his horse fed and rubbed down in the inn-yard and bade his servants pack and make haste. Together they rode out of Angers to the sound of the King's men fighting the Queen's men, but Kenelm Digby had no wish to be of either side. He hoped that the sentry would spread the word that he was indeed dead. Meantime, he would ride south, out of madame's reach. What an escape! And still soft, strong and warm about his arm was the long lock of Venetia's hair.

If Paris had been a disappointment and Angers a fiasco, Kenelm found that Italy set his mind afire. From the time he first rode down into the land of rough red wine and harsh voices—astonishing when they sang so beautifully!—he was set free to think, to ponder, to talk; especially in Florence, where the sparkling air above the running Arno contained a kind of heady spirit, affecting everyone he met besides himself. It was as if they all went a little mad while remaining sane in everyday things; but here so little was everyday, or if it was must be looked at, argued about, with a new fascination, a new insight. He found his Italian well remembered and grew increasingly fluent, practising it in taverns, in the street, in great palaces with baffling blank walls that hid the talents contained in them; talents of painting, of jewel-craft, of argument, logic and science.

The latter he had never been taught at Oxford for it was not on the curriculum, yet here it was almost common talk, and not far off was Professor Galileo Galilei himself, to whom Kenelm had a letter of introduction from Tom Allen. He would visit the great man soon, perhaps be allowed to look through his invention of the refractory telescope, perhaps even see the new moons of Jupiter Galilei had discovered, and above all hear him talk. But meantime he penned a note to his mother with one enclosed for Venetia, letting both women know that, despite talk of his death at Angers, he was alive and well, but not to make it known in France.

Mary Digby received the letters. She had not heard the rumour of Kenelm's death, deep as she remained in the country. His letter relieved her, but the enclosed one to Venetia she put in the fire and watched it burn. She would not permit her son's association with such a young woman to continue; Venetia Stanley's name was already bandied about with that of both Dorset brothers, the Earl himself and Edward Sackville, as even Mary had heard in her seclusion. Since the lost day in the forest her determination had in any case grown. If Venetia, in town, heard of Kenelm's death it was all to the good; she need not learn the contrary for some time.

As she came back from the fire Mary glimpsed herself in a mirror. Her mouth had grown mean and tight with loss of teeth, her eyes those of a dead woman. She passed her hand across them, remembering Everard. If he had lived, it would have been different; it would all have been different, and she not left alone to bring up two strapping sons unaided. Thankfully, Johnny wanted to be a soldier. He would be a good one; he knew how to obey orders.

But what was to become of Kenelm? Meantime, at any rate, he was engrossed in his travels, and he had also mentioned in his letters that he had been asked in Italy to give a lecture on certain writings of the ancients. Mary took the news levelly, as she did everything unexpected about Kenelm except his love for Venetia. Even in Spain he had begun to collect old wives' recipes for cookery and salves; such things interested him, and were harmless enough and would keep his mind from love until it was time for a suitable marriage.

In London, Venetia learned of Kenelm's death from Edward Sackville. Islip, having been slipped a guinea, had gone downstairs. The sounds from the street outside were as usual; cries of lavender-sellers, men crying the hours, dogs barking, footsteps hurrying on their different ways. Venetia was seated near the window twisting Kenelm's diamond ring on her finger. She was often glad of it; it reminded her that he was real, though absent, and his love constant as the stone gleamed. She hoped that he was still wearing her bracelet of hair.

Sackville had come into the room. She did not look at him with any curiosity; his presence in the house was so constant she had grown used to it. It took her some moments to realize that he was unusually quiet and had remained leaning against the door. "Well, Ned," she said absently, turning to him at last. He still looked grave, and came to her.

"It is evil news, sweetheart," he told

her, "and I would bring it to you gently. Attend me."

"About your brother?" She seldom thought of one without the other; they were always about her, both big fair men with lecherous eyes, one of whom had rescued her from the wolf. She had resisted frequent attempts from each to become her lover. But it was pleasant to have acquaintances about Court, who would bring her the news. She saw Sackville shake his head. He took her hand, holding it firmly.

"Not that, but the worse for you, I fear. Someone you love greatly is dead, killed in a fight at Angers."

"Kenelm?" He nodded. Venetia flung her free hand up against her mouth. All of a sudden it seemed as if her throat were full of tears, salt to the taste, and her eyes rained them on her cheeks unceasingly. "How—who—"

He was kissing her hand. "They say the young King's men, in a fight against his mother's guards. That is all we know." He began to kiss her forearm, then her upper arm, shoving up the linen. He was kissing her open mouth and throat. "Venetia . . .

beautiful, cruel Venetia . . . let me comfort you, I love you as much as any man ever did, I would have you for my own, my own . . ."

She still wept as he carried her to the bed. It did not seem to matter what he did with her. Kenelm, glorious Kenelm of the brown curly hair and immense strength, who had given her a crown of flowers and a diamond, was dead. That was all that mattered, all she could think of, all she must weep for; never any more to see Kenelm, to hear his rumbustious voice.

The tears flowed on. Sackville, within her at last, smiled to himself, and began to unlace her bodice. He had had a wager with Dick over this, concerning which of them should win her first. Now that he had won her, he would keep her for a while; only a while, until he made some successful marriage.

Presently, seeing her naked, he gently drew the diamond ring from her finger. Venetia sobbed on, hardly noting its absence, hardly caring; without Kenelm nothing meant much any more, and whoever would might have her, for what it was worth to them.

". . . and I must tell you something which will both surprise and please you, Messere Digby, with your knowledge of the parabola; namely, that a cord stretched more or less tightly assumes a curve which closely approximates that entity. The coincidence is the more exact if the parabola is drawn with less curvature or, so to speak, more stretched."

Professor Galileo Galilei's mild eyes sparkled behind their thick spectacles. It was the tragedy of this great man that he was slowly becoming blind; but already in his life had had perceived more truths than most men of average vision. Kenelm would always remember the long full white beard, the spotless linen collar, the expressive hands and tongue and the knowledge they revealed.

"Then," he said, anxious to retain the argument with one so exalted, "with a fine chain one would quickly be able to draw many parabolic lines on a plane surface. Indeed, as I shall demonstrate to you." The old man had put his hand to his ear

143

to catch the words uttered in Kenelm's resonant voice. He was going deaf as well.

Kenelm watched the production of the precisely curved lines, as he had looked through the famous telescope and while not able to see Jupiter's moons—they were not at this time of year in evidence—he had seen for himself the spots on the sun which Galileo had discovered and which had led him to deduce many shocking theories about the earth's certain movements round the sun. While remembering this, he said presently: "There is one thing I should be anxious to be convinced of; the statement that it is impossible by any force whatever to stretch a cord so that it will lie perfectly straight and horizontal."

"I will see if I can recall that demonstration," said the professor, smiling; this young man's enthusiasm cheered him after the displeasure of the Church authorities and the lassitude of some of his students. He laid his hand on the other's arm; what muscles, as well as brain! "In order for you to understand it, Digby, it will be necessary for you to take for granted, concerning some machines, what is evident not only from experiment but from theoretical considerations. I mean that the velocity of a moving body—even when its force is small—can overcome a very great resistance exerted by a slowly moving body, whenever the velocity of the moving body bears to that of the resisting body a greater ratio than the resistance of the resisting body to the force of the moving body."

"That is demonstrated by Aristotle, is it not?"

"He was right in some things."

"As you will know, sir, a counterpoise weighing not more than four pounds will lift a weight of four hundred provided that the distance of the counterpoise from the axis about which rotation exists be more than one hundred times as great as the distance between this axis and the point of support for the large weight."

"You are quite right, Digby. You do not hesitate to admit that however small the force . . ."

Kenelm's Italian servant tried not to yawn, for he could not understand a word, but was glad that his venturesome young master was happy; all the same they had been here three hours, and a man needed a drink. This old gentleman, the professor of mathematics, had had his share of troubles, evidently; but the delight with which he talked to the young master would cheer him.

It was curious to Kenelm's way of thinking that after visiting Galileo he should travel on to Rome, where the authorities had censured sunspots and made their discoverer abjure them meantime. Kenelm was received by the Pope, and they talked informally, with one aged cardinal in attendance; His Holiness remembered the death of Kenelm's father, for whom, with the other plotters, he had tried to intercede at the time. He talked at some length with Everard Digby's son. "It is hard to receive any news of England without prejudice one way or the other," said Paul V. Later they walked about the Sistine Chapel and gazed at a somewhat vapid *Adoration of the Magi* by a young Flemish painter named Anthony van Dyck. "You must meet that young man," the Pope told him. "He is not at his best in religious painting. I understand that his portraits are a different matter."

"They are somewhat flattering," said old Cardinal Bellarmine, "but that will please a great many people." He smiled above his long beard.

Kenelm bowed his way at last out of the company of the able Borghese prince who had boldly excommunicated Venice for impertinence, and from the man who had earlier refused the Papacy itself; he had been glad to feel Cardinal Bellarmine's hands on his head in blessing, as well as the Pope's. Once walking out among the new colonnades, he hastened to ask the direction of van Dyck's studio, for the painter had for the time left Genoa, where he resided, to live in Rome. Next day Kenelm visited the studio beside the yellow Tiber—how different from the clear-running Arno, and with so separate a history!—and found a small, dapper, courteous young man only a few years older than himself. Van Dyck seemed bent on advancement and was already gaining it; unfinished portraits of high-ranking churchmen and Roman nobility stood against the walls, and one of a white-haired man with a wise high-bred face stood almost ready on an easel. "You should come to England," said Kenelm. The painter made a small gesture of dissent.

"I have already been," he said. "I have painted your King James. He is not easy to paint with pleasure. And I painted the Countess of Arundel when she was in Germany. I travel much, you see." He surveyed the splendid young man before him; how he would like to paint that hair, and that physique! His teacher Rubens might have done better, however.

"I am not familiar with the Court," said Kenelm. "I live in the country when I am at home. My religion is against me."

"It will prosper you here," said the painter comfortably. He moved to the easel and its portrait, looking at the latter. "This makes me happier than a Papal commission," van Dyck went on. "The Marchese is to come at any moment for his sitting. Stay to meet him; he is a charming and influential personage, and will give you the entry to many great houses here, should you wish it."

Kenelm reflected that purely social calls did not interest him. They began to talk instead of chemistry, having discovered that it interested them both, and of the search for the Philosopher's Stone, not yet abandoned.

"Your old Queen Elizabeth they say paid a fortune to her alchemists to find it before she died, but they could not," said van Dyck. "The new methods are better. They say it is red; Paracelsus in his day and all the others since are agreed on that one thing, though some say it is flexible and others hard as rock. I do not know. But when I go back to Genoa, to my laboratory there, I will try again."

"Have you used quicksilver and brimstone, burning both?"

"Naturally. There is a red powder made from the first alone, but it has no properties in especial that I can find."

"Have you weighed the stuff before and after burning? Is it heavier or lighter? I am interested to know whether or not there is a substance in the air that is withdrawn from it under those conditions."

But the sound of the Marchese's coach came from the road, and both men broke off their talk and bowed low as he entered; he had a presence one could respect at sight, but talked easily and kindly to the two young men. Van Dyck arranged the pose, took up his brushes and began to apply swift strokes to the painting, walking back and forth across the expanse of floor.

"He must walk long distances, he is becoming so successful," jested the Marchese. "Have you yourself an interest in painting, Signore? A little, perhaps? You are interested in everything? That is well, for a young man. At my age one retreats into books."

They talked then of his library, which he kept in his *castello* beyond the city. "I have many books that would interest the signor," he said. "He must come and see them for himself."

The courtesy of the formal Italian flattered Kenelm. "I should be honoured," he said, and meant it. He loved books, constantly discovering some matter that had been lost for centuries; old recipes, an unknown and forgotten sonnet to translate, a musical score for the lute when he had time to play it as much as he had done in Oxford. And there was philosophy, both the ancient and new. He assented gladly to the suggestion that the Marchese's coach should come for him in some days' time, and although they had just encountered one another felt the old nobleman's constant regard as special in some way, as though oneself had been a favoured son. He left the painter and his model in the studio, where there was being set down a telling likeness of velvet, satin, rich lace and civilized humanity.

There were several English in Rome, and it so happened that Kenelm encountered one man whom he had known slightly at Oxford. They said little together about that place except that it seemed a pity no new thought ever came there, and Kenelm enquired for Tom Allen, who was growing old. After that the gossip turned to London. The King stank as much as ever and would bathe his legs after the hunt in a deer's warm blood to strengthen them; long-legged Villiers was increasingly a favourite since the disgrace and imprisonment of Somerset.

"They say the King can refuse George Villiers nothing, and the Prince of Wales hateth him accordingly," said Kenelm's acquaintance. "Now that he hath been made Marquis of Buckingham he will soon be one of the richest men in England. And all this from nothing, like Robin Carr when he first lay at the King's feet with a broken leg, and His Majesty was enchanted with his beauty!"

"Buckingham married money as well, I believe," said Kenelm.

"Ay, to Rutland's heiress. They say he was broken-hearted when Buckingham carried her off and must needs marry her afterwards because of the scandal. Rutland's own young heirs were both killed by witchcraft many years ago, and his daughter was all he had left."

They discoursed for some time about witches and their charms, and Kenelm was thinking already that if one charm could kill at a distance, another might cure. "No doubt a good marriage is a sensible thing in the general way," he said judicially. "I myself shall marry for love." His fingers closed over that part of his sleeve which hid Venetia's bracelet of hair. The other smiled a little.

"No one marries for love," he said, "they take the loved one for lover or mistress, and let the world look to its own. Ask Ned Sackville, who hath been dangling after Dame Venetia Stanley for long enough before getting his reward. Now they say he hath finally won her, though he will not marry her; I am told she is pregnant by him."

He tossed off his wine, oblivious of the silence.

"What proof have you of this?" said Kenelm's voice at last. Some change in it made the other look up. So it was true, was it, as they said, that Kenelm Digby had himself been enamoured of the fair Venetia?

"Ben Jonson writes verses to her," he said lamely, trying to atone. But Kenelm looked pale, as though the very life had gone out of him. The Englishman took his leave presently, aware that he had brought the most unwelcome news of all.

Left alone, Kenelm raged about the room; unwound the shining hair from his arm, cast it in the fire and watched it burn. The flame it made was blue and wan; the acrid, sulphurous smell filled the room. To such it had come, his love; stinking ashes. Henceforth he would be free; but meantime he cursed all women, and took to his bed for two days.

Some time later, the Marchese's coach was sent for him. He made himself rise, shave and dress; went down, and got in at the door, and let the coach rumble on its way. As it travelled on he settled down to his own reawakening thoughts, not remarking the road. He would go back presently to Florence, perhaps take a house there and stay for a while within sight and reach of the Duomo; meet the eager minds, join in the crisp, inviting talk; cook subtle dinners for his friends, afterwards hearing music or discussion on one or another subject far into the night. The mind had no boundaries. Already he was happier, at thought of it; almost as happy as he remembered being as a child, before his father had been taken from him. How greatly the events of his life had stemmed from that! But for it, he would never have loved as faithfully, as extravagantly, as exclusively. Now all that was over, and his life about to begin. But first he must visit the Marchese and see his library.

The Marchese's *castello* was set high in the mountains above Frascati, one aspect looking down on the bishop's palace, the other far out into the wrinkled blue of the Tyrrhenian Sea, with a ghostly jagged line on the horizon which might be the mountains of Sardinia. The great door had a carving of the Marchese's coat of arms above it in the yellow stone. Kenelm's host himself met him in the hall, which abounded in suits of armour, lovingly polished, of bygone ancestors who had fought in the Pope's wars.

"You will be weary after your journey," said the Marchese. "Perhaps you will like to go to your room and rest. I will have wine and food sent up to you. Afterwards we will play cards, if you wish." The wise glance Kenelm had already noted was again fixed on him; eyes almost opaque, brown and sad, yet glowing.

Next day Kenelm met his hostess, a woman of an old family, much younger than her husband, but evidently devoted to him; she was like certain paintings

Kenelm had seen in Spain, oval-faced, full-bosomed, with smooth dark hair and discreet eyelids. He was pleased that so young and attractive a woman should not be discontented up here; surely she longed for the society of her own generation? But his own bitterness about Venetia was eating at him; all women could not be like that, volatile, unfaithful. He began to draw the Marchesa out in talk, and found her responsive and intelligent, her husband looking on agreeably.

"My wife has no time to read in the library, but it is yours whenever you want it. Also, if you should desire to hunt in the forests, my *capocaccia* is yours tomorrow, and the dogs and horses: you may get a stag or two, and there are wild boar, but they are growing rarer."

"I will be content with reading," said Kenelm, bewildered by this display of lavish hospitality. What made the Marchese so kind to him, as if he were to inherit all his goods? Meantime he rejoiced in what he found in the leather-bound library, its bindings old and flaking now; obscure recipes, Church history, some plainchant in black letters which he could scarcely read; a herbal; various philosophers, and Aristotle and Copernicus; the travels of Ulysses and the wars of Troy, and a great-sized volume on the layout of gardens. He mentioned the latter to the Marchese when they met at dinner.

"Your plans for mazes would put ours in England to shame, and I have learnt much I did not know of herbs. There is so much knowledge concealed in that room that I believe I would be happy forever within its four walls."

"You would not; you have an active body as well as a seeking mind. Young men do not shut themselves away, unless they are monks, which would not suit you, my friend."

The long fingers crumbled walnuts over the wine; they were alone, the Marchesa having withdrawn, and the servants had left them together. The Marchese was looking at Kenelm intently, and suddenly the latter burst forth: "What is it you want of me? You have given me as much as if —as if I had been a saint, or a god, or your son." His words sounded loud in his own ear; the civilization of this great nobleman far exceeded his own or any he might meet with in England.

"But you will have noted, by now, that I have no son." The voice was sad, yet the papery lids raised themselves to reveal a glance deep with hope. "You have met my wife," the Marchese said, "and she likes you for yourself. I noted you, in the painter's studio, as a perfect physical specimen, of good blood, and during the past days I have found that your mind is not inferior. I have a favour to ask of you, if you will; to give my wife a child, as I cannot."

"Sir—" He had flushed; how was he to respond to the sincerity of the invitation? He reminded himself that before he had known of Venetia's infidelity, he would not have considered the matter. Now—

"You may take a little while to think of it; I do not force you. But it would give me pleasure to have a son of yours to inherit my ancient name: I have no other heirs. I am old, and would see him before I die."

"That must not be for long." Kenelm suddenly saw himself as another might see him; a brawny, raw, somewhat intellectual

Englishman, young enough to be startled, perhaps not worldly enough to be cynical, at such a suggestion. From the Marchese's viewpoint he could become what was required. From his own—

"My wife will not join us for meals in future," said the old voice gently, "but you will be conducted to her room at nights."

So it was. He was led by a stone lamp, swimming in oil as the Romans must have used them, to a wide carved door, and inside there was darkness and silence. The hush of the thick hangings veiled his footsteps as he made his way towards the bed. Once between the sheets, he found a woman's flesh; the first time he had possessed it, had dreamed of such possession. The flesh itself smelled sweet; there was nothing tarnished about this woman, nor did words pass between them. Sometimes he laughed at himself, remembering the legend of Cupid and Psyche and how he had forbidden her to have light that she might not see his face. But the thought of himself as Cupid was ludicrous; he justified himself, left his seed in her night after night and went back to his room; that was all.

By day he continued with his reading, and once or twice took out the hunt; the dogs' collars were more ornate than at home, with great iron studs surrounded by intricate leatherwork and great jewels of different colours, as well as gilding. They were large and fierce, perhaps descended without much change of blood from the mastiffs the ancient Romans had brought long ago to Britain. His host was always interested to hear of the day's hunt, but never asked about the night's reward. Only, one evening some months after Kenelm had come, while they sat together at dinner, the Marchese said quietly:

"My wife is with child. She is certain. I am infinitely obliged to you. Now I can die happy, having seen your son."

Next day Kenelm rode out of the *castello* and made his way to Florence. While still there, many months later, he received a letter from the Marchese at his town house in Rome.

My wife has given birth safely to a fine

son. He has brown curling hair. May God's blessing attend you.

By then, Kenelm had word that Sir John Digby wanted him again in Spain. The older man did not say why, but asked Kenelm to come urgently.

Your knowledge of the language, and your religion, make you a necessary part of our enterprise,

he wrote. Kenelm was intrigued; what enterprise?

He made a last journey into the Tuscan hills, for a plant which interested him for cookery would be already in flower, and he would cut it and dry it later in the sun from the balcony of his room. He had taken a last look regretfully at the familiar chamber in which by now he had lived for almost two years, whiling away the time reading, making music, writing verse, and lecturing to the *Filomati,* the Seekers, a society like himself interested in many things but sure of none.

The flasks and alembics he used for his

experiments would be easily broken, and he thought for a moment of sending them to his mother in England to keep for him. Perhaps, however, they might be bought elsewhere as cheaply. He set out, journeying in the cool of the early day; found his plants, plucked the flowers and leaves and stowed them in his saddlebag, and returning along the Pistoia road found himself thirsty, and stopped at an inn he knew and had visited once or twice: the landlord was a mean fellow, but his wine was good. Kenelm left his horse in the care of a ragged boy, and strode into the inn. He could hear loud words as soon as he reached the door, and a shabby figure was ejected roughly and sprawled in the roadway, his rope belt splaying in the dust.

"We want none of your begging folk here. A meal indeed! Those who eat meals here pay for them."

"Hold," said Kenelm, and knelt down by the prone man. His face was lined and almost black with the sun, and he seemed too weak to respond. "Bring wine," said Kenelm, and the landlord, who knew the Englishman was always ready with his money, brought some, carefully poured into a leather jack. "Drink, good brother," said Kenelm, holding up the friar's head; but the other turned away.

"I may not drink wine or eat meat. An egg perhaps, or a crust of bread . . . a drink of water . . . I have travelled far."

Kenelm ordered the bread and the water, and paid for them wordlessly. "If you treat a good friar so you will not prosper," he said to the man. After the friar had eaten and drunk he asked him which way he went; to Florence or to Bologna?

"To Florence. I have lately come from Bologna. There they were kinder, but it is the heat of the day." He had sat up, and passed a hand in a rough brown sleeve across his forehead. "I have to thank you," he said, but Kenelm cut him short.

"I do little enough. Do you mount my horse and I will lead him, and that will give you a rest from walking as far."

The friar mounted Kenelm's horse, which was a roan jennet the latter often used, and together they went on their way, Kenelm leading the horse. When he reached his own lodging he asked the friar to come in. "I can make you a meal of eggs, or whatever you will," he said. "It gives me pleasure to cook." And he broke the eggs and beat them up with some herbs, and cooked an omelette. He and the friar ate together, the good man blessing the food before they ate it.

"Do you come from far?" asked Kenelm. He knew the travelling friars often covered huge distances, but was impressed when the man said he came from China.

"Our monastery there is made out of rock, high above the plain. I came to bring certain knowledge to my brothers in Florence and in Rome, but I was robbed on the way, and my scrolls are gone."

He moved, turning his shaved head from the table to where the alembics jutted, their long spouts catching the evening sunlight with its dusty motes. "You have been a Good Samaritan to me," the friar said, "and you are a man who seeks knowledge. In thankfulness I will give you a secret known to few, and to none, I believe, yet in the West. Would it please you to have it?"

"What is it, good brother?" He was of

164

course interested, any new thing was always welcome; and when he heard more he was ecstatic, and went for a quill and paper.

"It will cure many things even though the wound, or the ill, is at a distance," said the friar. "It is called the Powder of Sympathy."

"I have heard of it." Someone at the Filomati had mentioned it, but had not known more except that its powers were famous. Was it more fanciful than to cure warts in a slice of bacon turned south by a window, or holding one's hands in a silver basin full of moonbeams? He listened, and wrote.

"Some say it is necessary to have the grease of a dead man's head. It is not. There is a harsh salt of sweet vitriol, and a volatile salt which it catches within itself, which is the essential part of the cure. The atoms of the air as you will know travel in currents, and will follow a straight line unless they are drawn off their natural course." Kenelm thought of Galileo and his weights and forces. "A strong influence, like a magnet, or fire, will draw them aside. A siphon will do it also. Atoms of a

165

like kind are the more readily attracted to one another. Thus a burned hand will be attracted by fire, and the wound will feel better in the heat of it."

"Is that why a viper's bite may be cured by holding the snake with its mouth open over the wound it made, as you will know?"

"I have no knowledge of that. Atoms of one kind are in general attracted by some similar matter. And the lesser number will always be drawn to the greater. A fire sucks light to itself from open doors and windows."

"The principle of sympathy must control much of life."

"In my opinion, everything. When you find a wounded man, try the powder, after adding water in a certain measure and dipping a knife-blade into the mixture until it comes out copper."

"I am grateful."

"You must be careful. In the wrong hands this knowledge could do great harm."

"I will let none have it whom I cannot trust."

"Ah, you trust too many," sighed the

friar. Next day Kenelm saw him on his way, and returned with excitement to the notes he had made regarding the Powder of Sympathy, which he would take with him into Spain, and study them there.

4

KENELM had determined not to travel on mule-back from Barcelona, as his cousin had spoken of their meeting in Madrid as urgent. Instead he went to some trouble, after the ship docked, to find out a horse; but this was so difficult that in the end he was forced to try one offered by a disagreeable fellow who insisted on accompanying him into the mountains.

"My horse is valuable. There are *ladros* in the hills." Kenelm was aware of this, for the thieves on either side the road, hiding in the uneven scrub, were notorious. However he had brought nothing of value with him except a little money, and unwillingly rode off at last on the man's nag, while the owner followed him on another. They rode on in silence, making speed enough; the high sierras were still covered with snow, and the wind was very cold. Kenelm heard, as they rode on out of the straggling port and into the hills, the hungry cry of a wolf; he fired his pistol to keep the beast away and also to let the sullen Spaniard know he was armed.

The wind rose, keening down the valleys, and it grew bitterly cold although the month was already March. Presently a flake of snow brushed like a feather against Kenelm's cheek, then another and another; soon it was snowing in thick flurries, beginning to lie in whorls on the road where the wind had whipped it. Kenelm set his head down and urged his horse, hearing at last, over the howling of the wind, the whirr and click of Castilian oaths behind him. "What is it?" he shouted above the blast, turning his head. The man dismounted and came to Kenelm's bridle. "We cannot go on in this storm," he muttered, as though others listened; he had this constant aspect of guilt about him, and Kenelm wondered if he were in league with some of the robbers and if he himself would now be set upon.

"I may not return," he said firmly. "I have business in Madrid."

"Then you must make your way by yourself, for I will not lose the horse in this snow. He is valuable, you hear me?"

"He will safely be left at the next post-ing-inn."

"There is no inn for miles. I am taking him back with me. If the señor wishes to return on him he may do so. Otherwise he will have to make his own way on foot. *Madre de Dios,* I will be glad to reach Barcelona!"

Kenelm tried to proffer a gold coin, of which he only had a few; but although the Spaniard looked at it covetously he shook his head. "My horse is worth more," he insisted.

"How much is the damned nag worth, that I may buy it?"

"I will not sell him. He is worth much, much money. He earns my living for me." I daresay, thought Kenelm, who had already paid for the hire of the horse. He cursed his folly in not joining a mule-train. Perhaps one would pass; in the meantime it was useless to stand and argue with this fellow in the wind and cold. He dismounted, flung the reins to the man, and saw him disappear into the whirling whiteness.

Taking his saddlebag in his hand, Kenelm plodded on. Surely, on this road, someone would pass other than robbers; and the latter would not find much. He was glad of his strength, for the bag was heavy and the wind blew the snow hard against him; soon he was soaked to the skin through his thick clothing, his hat's brim sodden and dripping water down his neck. He had never felt so uncomfortable, and had it not been for Sir John and his urgency would have turned aside and sought shelter in such cover as he might find. The ground was beginning to grow impassable with the drifting of the snow, and between the flurries he could see the occasional stone pine, leading to forests.

It was when he was about to shelter behind one of these that he heard a sound which was different from the moaning of the storm. He clutched his hat and looked round. A curious effect came to him; that a solid wall of snow was moving towards him, making greater speed than he did; then he made out mounted bearers, and realized that the equipage was a litter, hung all in white. One of the bearers dismounted and came to him courteously.

"My master greatly desires speech with you," he said in Spanish. Kenelm was in such misery that he would have talked with the devil. He made his way to the litter, which had stopped; at the same time thinking that this personage, for such it must be, was well guarded against *ladros.* If he could, he must travel with his party.

The white curtains were already parted for him; afterwards he was to find that they were of silk so tightly woven that the wind and wet could not penetrate it. Out of the snow, a notable face could be seen, hooded in white. The eyes were dark and gentle, the skin pale; the fingers which held the curtain aside were long, slim and well-kept.

"My friend," said the strange man, "you will never reach Madrid on foot in this weather, and we are far from any inn. Would it please you to ride in my litter with me?" He spoke in English and Kenelm was astonished that someone knew of his identity; how had the man discovered it? But that could wait. He thanked the unknown gentleman profusely, and climbed into the litter. Inside were cushions, embroidered inner curtains, and a small brazier which gave off a comfortable warmth and which was not even blown by the wind where it sat sheltered by the draperies in a corner of the floor.

Kenelm sat down at his host's request. He had taken off his hat and the wet plastered his hair to his face; he was aware of the figure he must present, and apologized. "It is the fault of the weather, not yours, my friend," replied the stranger in even tones. Kenelm opened his saddlebag and took out a linen towel, drying his neck and ears and taking off his cloak to dry; the interior was warm enough.

The litter had started to travel again with its even, rocking motion. He did not like to ask the name of his host before it was offered; seeing the man clearly now, it was evident that he was old. Yet his pale skin was unwrinkled and his features fine-drawn. He was clothed all in white; beneath the full robes his slippers were of white leather. It was evident that he had not set foot on the foul roads of Spain.

"Sir," said Kenelm, "my curiosity invades my manners. How did you know I was an Englishman? How do you protect yourself from the weather in places such as this? It reminds me of Venice, where one may walk with thin silk shoes and hose without ever soiling them, the streets are so clean. But that is not the case here."

His host smiled. "As regards your first question, I make it my business to know such things," he said. "In any case my servant reported two horses returning, one without a rider. I instructed him to stop you when you were seen and to offer you a place in my litter."

Deliberately, Kenelm crossed himself. "Your faith is not unlike my own," said the traveller. "In the beginning was the Word, and the Word was Brahma."

"I have heard of your faith," said Kenelm to the swaying of the litter. In fact one of the Filumati members had been much interested in Brahmanism and had read a paper concerning it. "You have your Trimurti, we our Trinity."

"Brahma, Vishnu, Siva. And from Brahma's head sprang the Brahman, the twice-born. Below us are the princes the Kshatriyas; they came from the arms of Brahma, and again from his thighs came the husbandmen, the Vaisyas; and last of all, from his feet, the Sudra."

"And the rest of mankind?"

"They are outcasts. But that does not prevent my giving you a comfortable journey on an uncomfortable road." The smile remained, and the eyes, wise and dark with great kindness in them, reminded Kenelm of the Marchese watching him over wine and walnuts at the *castello*. He was fascinated with this Brahman; all knowledge seemed to be at his command. "Do you then believe that all things happen other than by chance?" he said. "I had begun to think of my own life as a series of bitter coincidences, with no pattern to them."

"There is a pattern in everything," said the Brahman. "When you are as old as I am you will be able to look back and perceive that it is true. But what troubles you so, a young man with the world before him, possessing everything but a horse?"

"I am not possessed of a return for true love. I was faithful to a woman who has been unfaithful to me, and now I am bitter, and cannot forgive her or myself, for my own folly."

The wind had dropped. The Brahman put his long fingers to the curtain again, and drew it aside carefully. The snow had gone, and they were travelling along a road where pines and oak trees grew on either side, shading the way. "Let us alight here for a little while," the Brahman said. From the folds of his robe he brought out a little book, covered in lead, and gave it to Kenelm. It had leaves made of soft unborn lambs' skin, and on them were engraved curious signs and pentacles. Kenelm, bringing all his knowledge of such things to bear, could understand only some of them.

They had alighted. The bearers also dismounted and went off in turn to relieve themselves. Kenelm became aware of his own need, but out of courtesy waited till the older man should have revealed whatever it was he wanted him to understand. They walked on together till they came to a clear place where a fallen oak lay, long rotten. The air was still; it did not seem possible that so short a time and distance ago there had been bitter cold, wind and storm.

The Brahman's lips and hands were moving. Slowly Kenelm became aware of a third presence whom at first he could not see. Within moments, however, a whiteness appeared nearby the fallen oak; and almost crystallized, or so he saw it, into the figure of a woman, brooding and sorrowful, veiled from head to foot, the bright hair lying on her shoulders, her fair arms empty. The long fingers and the averted face were those of Venetia.

He stepped forward, as if he were in a dream. He wanted to touch the apparition, but when he went to take her hand she vanished, and he was left staring at the empty oak. Bewildered, he turned to the Brahman, but there was nobody there; the man had gone a little way off, and waited till Kenelm came up to him, smiling. The young man was pale and distraught. "What does it mean?" he asked. "How could she come here?"

"I bade my spirit bring her. You will see that she mourns for you. She thinks that you are dead."

"But I sent a letter—to her and to my mother—"

Suddenly he knew the truth, or part of it. He found himself trembling. The vision had seemed real enough. But was it true, or a mere figment of what this strange man called his spirit?

"I tell you also that in a few days you will fight armed men, but will overcome them."

They returned to the litter, and continued on the journey to Madrid, where Kenelm left his benefactor with many grateful words and blessings. He himself was happier than he had been for long, owing to the vision, and the possibility that after all Venetia might still love him. But events were to prevent his writing to her immediately; on arrival at the house John Digby had taken in Madrid, there was much else to think of, and no leisure. The prospect, if it were true, of the fight did not trouble Kenelm; the Brahman had promised that he would win.

"How welcome you are, Kenelm!" said the new Earl of Bristol, himself opening the door that led out to the windy Madrid street. Kenelm followed his kinsman into a lighted room where a great Austrian stove blazed, its flames tossed about and flattened by the draught down the chimney. He went and warmed his hands at it, thankfully, while the servants took away his hat and cloak. He had been about to launch forth on the story of his journey, remembering the old Brahman by now as almost met with in a dream; but the sight of John Digby's altered face silenced him. The man had grown old, despite the earldom King James had lately given him in recognition of his services in trying to make peace within Europe, in Brussels and Vienna. His hair was grey, his face much lined, and his movements had slowed to a kind of constant deliberation, as if he were far older than his years.

"How fare you?" asked Kenelm gently, saying nothing after all of himself.

"Well or ill, as the days go; one never knows what news will come. I believe King James regrets his daughter's marriage to the Palatine and the war it brought when they claimed Bohemia; now everything is at sixes and sevens, and the least of it is that the family will not be let return to Heidelberg, for the Emperor holds it now as his own to bestow. Yet I must not distress you with ill news at the outset. It is a pleasure to see your handsome face, flushed with the wind as it is. There is a meal waiting for you; the maids have kept it on the spit. Before that you shall have wine, to warm yourself. Have you travelled far today?"

They sat by the stove and drank Spanish *rioja*, Kenelm feeling the chill in his limbs and body soon dispelled by it, by the heat, and by his kinsman's welcome. The Earl smiled to hear the story of the young man's journey for part of the way in a covered litter. "I did not think you had reached that stage," he said. Kenelm laughed, and decided not to tell his cousin the story of the vision he had seen; the practical statesman would mock at it, and Kenelm did not want it mocked. It would be a matter he would keep to himself meantime, perhaps for many years. He found himself listening instead to Bristol's doubts about King James's wish to right the balance in Europe by marrying his surviving son Charles, Prince of Wales, to the Spanish Infanta, sister to the new King Philip IV.

"The Spaniards will not have it on any count unless the Prince becomes a Catholic, and he himself is firmly set against that, willing as he is for the marriage," said the Earl. "I doubt if the

English nation would endure a Catholic king again, and although the King of Spain hath given way on certain points insisted on by his late father, we are still no further in the matter than we will ever be; I doubt me it is a coil that winds close to its end."

Kenelm would have answered, but there came a loud knocking on the outer door, and above the wind an English voice shouted: "Let me in, damn you, Bristol! Let me in! Let me in!"

The Earl frowned. "Whoever it is hath few manners," he said, and sent for his servant this time to open the door. Out of the windy night there swept in a tall bearded figure in a hat and cloak, the former of which he pulled off, shaking it free of wet, to reveal a head of close-curled dark hair. He grinned, got himself to the stove and stood before it, keeping the warmth from the other two men.

"A glass of your wine, I pray you, Bristol, my lord," he said, and his voice held both mockery and contempt. Bristol sitffened, and did not pour the wine.

"To whom have I the honour of speaking?" he asked coldly. The tall man broke into a roar of laughter.

"Tom Smith I have been, for the journey. If you know me not, Bristol, I must have had success where they did not know me so well. I am not an earl like your good self, merely a marquis. We passed by your messenger in Bayonne." He bowed a little, and mockery rose like a wall between the two men. Kenelm stared at the incomer's long legs, encased in fine leather sodden with the storm. "My lord of Buckingham," he heard Bristol say suddenly. "What do you in Madrid?" There was no welcome in the words. The other continued to smile his insolent smile, which seldom left his face.

"Why, I am here as Tom Smith, as I told you, having travelled with my coz, John Smith, here through France, and we saw fair ladies there, the Queen the fairest of all. I would I had Anne of Austria under me in a bed; I'd break down her Spanish stiffness better, I swear, than that popinjay she was married to. If Louis XIII had been a man, would she not have borne children ere this?"

"Where is your kinsman John Smith?" asked Bristol suddenly. His brows had drawn together in a close frown of great anxiety. Surely it could not be that Buckingham had brought another, a far greater other, on this mad venture, and that the King in Whitehall knew of it? Yet it would be typical of the man.

Buckingham laughed, went over to where the wine was and poured himself a glass without invitation, quaffed it off, and wiped his mouth with his sleeve. "John Smith is without, holding the horses," he said lightly. The Earl hurried to the door. Kenelm was left with the visitor, not liking him, yet in a way admiring his cool insolence; that, and his good looks, were what had raised George Villiers to the place he held today, King's favourite and, after long and bitter enmity between them, that of the Prince of Wales as well, who by now would do anything Buckingham bade him. One had heard of that even in Italy. But surely John Smith could not be the Prince of Wales himself, here in disguise in Spain? The notion was fantastic, almost impossible.

Yet the Earl returned, having left the horses with the grooms, and ushering in a smaller figure than that of Buckingham, one with a quiet dignity even in these

183

circumstances, his oval face likewise disguised by a heavy beard, his short legs encased in plain riding-boots, his plumed hat sodden.

"I bid your Royal Highness welcome to my house," said Bristol stiffly. The Prince smiled his rare, winning smile. "It is a pleasure to be here, my lord," he said: and then, with his trace of a Scottish accent still lingering, and a hint of the well-known stammer: "Steenie, man, g-get away from in front of the fire; others are clemmed besides yourself."

The visit might be an embarrassing one—King Philip's advisers had been horrified when they heard that the heretic Prince of Wales had appeared in person—but the Spaniards paid out their hospitality, which they could barely afford, with an air. For a few days Charles and Steenie were permitted to rest themselves from their journey at the Earl of Bristol's house, known to everyone as the House of the Seven Chimneys; then there was the triumphal entry into the city. Kenelm had to buy himself a new coat, so grand was everybody, in particular Buckingham, sparkling with jewels even to the heels of his shoes; privately Kenelm thought this display in bad taste. He was a jumped-up personage, was Steenie; and went out of his way to be offensive to Bristol, for no reason except that he was jealous of him as ambassador.

John Digby pursed his grave lips and said little, even to Kenelm. The procession took place, the Prince riding by King Philip, both of them, fair and dark, magnificent and well-seated in the saddle; the King spent most of his time on other days hunting, and Prince Charles, who had as a child of seven only just learned to walk, had forced himself by sheer effort of will since then to become an outstanding rider of the great-horse. His pale oval face, shorn at last of the disguising beard, and his gentle dignity drew cheers from the Spaniards, who by now disliked Buckingham for his familiar manners; it was whispered that he had made dishonourable gestures to two noblemen's wives already.

He rode with head in air, however, thinking this triumph his own and not Digby's; what had the new Earl done to earn his title except write more and more letters home? This visit would clinch the Spanish marriage. As for the Infanta, she was seen beside Queen Isabel, grown sadder-faced; both ladies dressed in brown velvet overlaid with much gold, and jewelled plumes in their broad-dressed hair. The Infanta had beautiful hair, curling and of an apricot colour; in fact it was her only beauty, though her pale complexion and jutting underlip marked her a Hapsburg. But the Prince, they said, was taken with her; soon everything would be as it should. The very sun shone brightly, the crimson-coated guard strutted, and trumpets sounded as they entered cold, shadowy Madrid.

"I do not make very much headway with the Archbishop of Toledo," Kenelm confessed to his cousin. Bristol smiled wearily; the past weeks had been full of slights, though not to himself. "Come, Kenelm, you are what is badly needed here, an English Catholic who speaks the tongue. And you are of good blood, and the Archbishop himself is only a young man. You should deal well together."

"He talks more to me of converting the

Prince than he does of youth or manners. And the Prince will never listen; I myself would not try to force him. He looks gentle, but he is stubborn, and set in the Church of England's mould already."

Bristol said in a low voice: "The marriage will never take place unless he does change. They cannot understand that in England, but it is evident to any peasant in the street here. King Philip's Gondomar and our Buckingham—" he grimaced over the name—"made this mad ploy between them, but the more serious-minded of the ministers here, such as Olivarez, know well enough that despite all the junketings, which they can ill afford—"

"They enjoy the junketings as well as we. At the bullfight there were thousands of spectators."

"Maybe; I like not the cruelty," said the Earl, who was ahead of his time. "They are paying clearly for this unasked visit and have responded with Spanish pride. But we are no longer in the days of Philip II when gold and silver flowed unchecked from the Indies into Spain. The Dutch have taken much of the market—"

"Dear sir, leave these heavy matters for

a while and divert yourself. Yours was the only long face in the procession, among the guards turned out in splendour and the great ruffs worn for the occasion."

"They even went to that expense in their laundry-bills, despite the law."

"Well, maybe things would go differently if the Prince could once speak to the Infanta for himself. It is summer now, and the two have not yet had other than formal words together, with the courtiers present and her ladies."

"That is Spanish etiquette. It would be perilous to try to overrule it."

But to overrule etiquette was exactly what the next escapade did.

Kenelm had made fast friends with the Prince of Wales, despite the overriding presence of Buckingham, who resented anyone but himself about the small slender young man. Kenelm admired Charles for his courage—he was as unlike his father in this way as any man could be—and for his informed mind on certain matters; he had read much, especially in those invalid years of his childhood exiled from Court, or else in the shadow of the brilliant elder brother who had so unexpectedly died, leaving Charles heir to the throne.

He did not, like many young men of his day, try his hand at verse; he had enough sense to know that his talents did not lie in that direction. But he had a great appreciation of beauty, and much admired the paintings in the palace King Philip had lent him in Madrid, and the splendour of the Court costumes, expensive though they might be. He asked Kenelm if he could teach him a little Spanish, and daily they had a session of it, though Charles's halting tongue lagged behind his brain. One day he sat smiling.

"We will soon have a chance to try this Spanish with the Infanta." Till now the young couple had used an interpreter, and the talk had accordingly been stiff and precise.

"Why," murmured Kenelm, "how will you contrive it?"

"Steenie has th-thought of a way." And the smile broadened to include his friend, who was further back in the room, impatiently picking at his nails till the lesson should have been completed. Buckingham could not live long without gaiety and the company of women, and spending money; he had run King James into thousands of pounds for debt already since the Spanish adventure had begun, trailing them through France. Now he rose, stretched to his full height, and said scornfully: "Is Digby to accompany us?"

"Why, yes; we cannot do without him lest we fail in a phrase, and in any case his company is welcome." Kenelm flushed with pleasure, and Buckingham dropped his eyelids. "Best tell him, then," he said to Charles, omitting any title.

The plan was to surprise the Infanta in the palace garden when she went out to gather May dew. The small party of men rose very early, attired themselves in clean linen and neat plain jackets, and set out to the wall they would have to climb, which led to the orchard. "I can hear the ladies come," whispered Steenie. Charles laid a finger to his lips, and nimbly scaled the wall. Kenelm followed, and while still some feet from the ground on the other side was in time to witness what happened.

He could see the Infanta, a small white-clad figure with her curly hair in undress

—and much more inviting than when it was frizzed, he thought—standing like a doll, her hands raised in outrage, while her attendants clustered round to screen her from the gaze of Charles, who was deep in a bow and had even essayed a few halting words of Spanish. An old grandee, his face anxious, hurried forward.

"You must go," he said in English. "If Your Royal Highness were found here by the guards they are instructed to cut intruders to pieces. We should not like that; please go, quickly."

Kenelm helped Charles back over the wall, lending his strong grip to heave the light weight up. They left the Infanta standing stiffly among the beds of ixias and forced tuberoses, and the darkening fruit-blossom of the orchard.

That escapade caused much scandal, and had pleased nobody, least of all the Prince, who had been made to feel foolish and who had not enough sense of humour to endure it. For the first time it was evident to him that the present impasse could go on and on, with no result other than loss of all dignity. At last he came to Bristol's house without Buckingham, and the two men were closeted for nearly an hour before the Prince emerged with tight lips. "Wait on His Royal Highness, Kenelm," his cousin directed, and Kenelm did so, but found Charles silent and moody on their return to the palace. He did not try to draw him out in talk, knowing, as Buckingham would not have done, that Charles Stuart needed to withdraw himself in silence to solace his own hurt pride.

Kenelm himself had meantime not been without adventures of his own. The first had been a fight, entered into on what was almost his first night in Madrid after the arrival of the royal visitor. He had gone out into the town with other young Englishmen including a kinsman, for about two hundred had followed the Prince's party, arriving in groups at different times into the now overcrowded capital. Three of them had broken off and had espied a young woman singing at her window, and her voice was so sweet that they had stopped to listen, even venturing a little nearer to view her where she shone in pale night attire, her hair loose.

At once there was a scuffle and some oaths, and a party with swords surrounded them; not adept, fortunately, but bristling with outraged honour. Kenelm drew his sword out, thankful for the moonlight; because of it, he saw the men who came at him; there were perhaps fifteen against only three English, including his own servant. He saw one, his cousin Lewis Dyve, strike hard with his blade at the helmet of the leader, but Lewis's blade snapped off at the hilt. He turned and ran.

Kenelm was dimly aware of his servant behind him, to whom the same had happened; the man was fighting with only the stub left. Sharp pain came to Kenelm suddenly and he felt the wetness of blood run down his hand; there would be a scar to show for it, if he lived; so far, few had fallen, and none of their own. He felt rage rise and with it, mighty strength; he backed into a narrow passageway, fighting all the time, and presently only one at a time could reach him; triumphant, he heard metal ring as one after another fought with him and fell, or else stepped back. The joy of his own great strength, his superior height and physique, came to him; he knew he was fighting like a god, and wielded the good sword bravely, left and right. By now, shutters had been flung open and heads stuck out into the night; a woman screamed; the moonlight was like full day, and, Kenelm remembered thinking grimly, this was better than a bullfight, but maybe much the same, with one man against all. He laughed suddenly; why were they fighting? "I do not know your lady," he called out in Spanish. "Villain, thou liest," was the answer, and the swords rang on.

There was nothing to do in the end but cut a way through; Kenelm lunged with his sword, but the Spaniard's coat was of leather. By sheer weight he bore the man down, and using him as a bridge over the bodies of those fallen so that the House of the Seven Chimneys came in sight, made for it, still keeping the fight in view with his head turned. There was a man coming after him, though, and his sword was raised high.

Kenelm side-stepped, and gave a great blow downwards at the man's head, which was bare as he had lost his helmet in the fight. The force of the blow split his skull and his brains flew out, as Kenelm said afterwards, into the next man's face. Kenelm slewed about, seized the dying Spaniard's sword, and ran it into the place between jack and soft belly; the man dropped, groaning, then lay dead. The rest had drawn back already from this gigantic and enraged Englishman, and skulked off. Kenelm wiped his blade and his hand, and went thankfully on towards the House of the Seven Chimneys.

The news of the fight went all about Madrid. It was evident that a mistake had been made, and so the matter was carried no further by the embarrassed hosts of English royalty: the band had set out to kill a rival lover of the lady by arrangement, and had thought Lewis Dyve the man. A certain Donna Anna Maria Manrique, who had often seen Kenelm at Court, not with indifference, sighed with pride when she heard the news; her big strong Englishman had put them all to the sword, had avenged his own honour! She was torn between love of him and the remembrance of her own high blood; her brother was a Duque and much in the King's company.

The news reached London, and in time Venetia heard it, wistfully knowing for certain now that Kenelm lived; how could she ever have doubted it? But she had lost him forever, even if it would have been possible to deceive him formerly; now, she sat here alone, great with child by Sackville, tears rising in her much-praised eyes and spilling down her face.

Kenelm was returning with the rest from a hunt in the summer woods of Valladolid, and his horse was weary and so was he. The hunt had been tame; the boars were fenced over a wide area, and one in particular had given so game a chase that by the end, stuck by many spears, he had run a quarter-mile with the blood spurting red from his wounds like a fountain, then dropped dead. For the first time Kenelm had thought of the cruelty of the chase, even though he had thrilled to the old sound, which he could remember from his father's time, of wound horns in the morning.

Kenelm thought now of his father, then

made his mind switch to the two matters that had interested him recently; he had taken to frequenting a Benedictine monastery for confession, to be out of the way of the Spanish Court with its tattle, and there he had encountered a deaf monk who had taught him lip-reading. It diverted him by now to be able to watch any pair at a distance and see what they were saying. So far he had learned nothing against himself, or even against the English party, though their hosts would surely tire of them by the end.

The second subject was his beloved cookery, and he had culled several receipts here in unexpected places; one for a tortilla of calves' brains with parsley, which he had written down and would use when he got home; another mixing chicken and fish, which he thought strange.

He was musing on it, when several of the rest, led by one Henry Rich who was kin to the famous Penelope, rode up. Rich began to jibe at Kenelm; they were friends enough to tease one another. "See him ride there, with never a thought for the ladies! The fairest ornament at Court came to watch us ride off in the morning, and he did not even smile at her. Perhaps his heart is cold."

"My heart is warm enough," retorted Kenelm, defenceless without the trust he had once had in Venetia to protect him from anything of the kind. "Which ornament?"

"Which ornament! There is only one; the fair Aña Maria herself. Hearken to this, sir," as the Prince rode up, followed by Buckingham, splendid on his bay hunter. "Your Royal Highness shall judge as to which of us wins her favour first; myself or this fellow here, Digby, who says his heart is warm. I can beat him on all counts, I believe."

"Well, try if you will," said the Prince, somewhat gravely, as if he himself had no heart for such a wager. He had been prepared to love the Infanta, but she continued to repulse him, and it could not be long now before his father lost patience and ordered his return to England. Let the pair play their game, accordingly; it could not last, even though Bristol had named the wedding day and ordered coats of pale blue velvet for the attendants. The wedding would not take place; Charles knew it.

Kenelm and Rich vied with one another, therefore, in trying for the heart of Doña Aña Maria Manrique. Kenelm, as always when he took on any matter, gave it his full mind and strength; and shortly there was gossip about the marked attentions of the large Englishman to the sister of the Duque de Maqueda. If she made a short journey by chair, Kenelm walked beside it; he even followed her to church, giving her more attention than he gave the altar; he was by her at the tilt, wearing her colours, even dressing his servants in them. He made eyes at her all through the Court entertainments, the masques where he would dance with her, the comedies by Lope de Vega; and Doña Aña began to respond, which was not etiquette.

In fact she had been secretly in love with Kenelm for a long time, and now it seemed as if he returned her love, which brought her great joy. Kenelm had no notion of the harm he was causing; he regarded the lady as a target to be hit as near the centre as possible, no more. As for Henry Rich, he withdrew from the lists quite soon. He and the other young Englishmen watched the romance with amusement, wondering how Digby would continue to deal at home with a Spanish wife.

One day Lewis, who had been in the affray, chaffed him on the matter. Kenelm was horrified. How would his mother take this, she who had permitted him to travel abroad until he should decide to come home and quietly wed a bride of her choosing? And he was not in the least in love with Doña Aña. Indeed he could never love again. He began to avoid the lady, which brought her great grief and almost resulted in a challenge to Digby from her brother the Duque. But King Philip advised against it; the English would go soon; he had private word from his ambassador in London. The excuse made was that a papal dispensation would be necessary, and it never came and, privately, never would come now.

Whitehall bade the Prince return at last,

and Charles took himself off as gracefully as it might be done, while Bristol was called to a special interview with the King. Philip's lack-lustre eyes for once held interest and regret. "You have made many friends here, and have carried out your task with devotion," he said. "It is not my personal wish that there should be estrangement, let alone war, between us." Buckingham in his wild way had talked of reopening the war with Spain as revenge for his banishment; he was one Englishman of whom the Spaniards, from highest to lowest, were glad to be rid. But Bristol's grave honest gaze reassured the King without words spoken. Philip drew a great jewel from his finger. "It is my wish that you wear it," he said, "and remember me."

So they parted, and never met again. As Bristol's party prepared to take ship at Santander, a letter was handed to Kenelm. It was from Doña Aña. She would never forget him, would love him always, and had entered a convent.

As for Kenelm, he caught smallpox.

He lay in bed at Gothurst, weary to the

bone, the crusts already dropping from his face, which would not be much marked; but the disease had tired him out and had left him without even a vestige of curiosity. Mary Digby hovered near the fire with a posset which she hoped he would take; it had been difficult to feed him through the fever and the recollection of strongly flavoured Spanish dishes. She was so glad to have him back, now the girls were married and away and Johnny busy about the estate awaiting a call to arms, that she fussed over Kenelm and did not mention any marriage project while he was ill. On the other hand she rejoiced in having some adverse news to give him of Venetia Stanley.

"They say she hath two children now by Sackville, I should say the fourth Earl, for his brother Dorset is dead of venery. But *she* will never be made his Countess. A virtuous woman would have held him off, and gained the title. She hath made herself a scandal and a mockery. You are well rid of her."

Kenelm felt tears rising in his eyes, and said weakly: "You are cruel, my mother. Venetia had no one to champion her; the

Dorset brothers took advantage of her while her father remained a slave to his books, and I was elsewhere."

"Well, that is as may be. By heaven, here is a rider." And she went to the window, leaving Kenelm to sup the bland posset she had prepared. He felt already that he would be glad to get back to good red meat; but, after Spain, life seemed unadventurous.

His mother's voice recalled him. "The rider bears the royal colours. Pray Heaven it is not more trouble." Mary still lived in the old days of the Gunpowder Plot, arrests, uncertainty, torture and execution. She put a hand to her mouth and ran down the stairs.

She returned with a letter for Kenelm. "Open it," she said anxiously. He did so, and presently his face broke into a smile. "Mother, the King wants to create me knight for supposed services in Spain. This must be Bristol's doing. I did nothing there except talk with an archbishop, who did not greatly like me, and by no means did I prosper the royal match."

She had snatched the letter from him, reading it close, for her eyes were not what

203

they had been. "It is perhaps in some way a reparation for your father's death," she said. At once Everard's memory came to her and her eyes filled with tears. What title could ever compensate for so deadly a loss? But Kenelm was talking gently.

"I must ride into Leicestershire; His Majesty and the Prince are there. I will be glad to see the Prince again." He remembered Charles, with his gentle dignity which had overcome the folly of the Spanish adventure.

"You will ride nowhere yet," said Mary. "You are not well."

"Madam, I shall do so. Can I refuse the King? And it will be good for all of us; it shows that his anger is no longer directed against us. I have no doubt that Bristol hath done his part for me, but it shows that the King no longer harbours resentment, does it not?"

"It will not bring back your father."

He threw back the covers, got up and went and kissed her. "What's past is past," he said. She stared at him as though he had been a stranger. Who was he to know of her agony, the bitter years since?

Kenelm could speak lightly of the whole thing, as if it were one more enterprise.

He rode into Leicestershire, and after the hunt there knelt in a clearing before an ageing, weak-legged man with a grey beard, with the Prince and Buckingham by him. The two latter he knew well enough, and that Buckingham had made so much trouble for his own kinsman Lord Bristol that the latter could not be present. But Kenelm received the stroke of King James's sword on his broad shoulder, and was dubbed knight. His Majesty shut his eyes at sight of the trembling blade he held; he had always a terror of naked steel, implanted in him when he lay in his mother's womb long ago at the murder of Rizzio. The blade wobbled and almost put out Kenelm's eye, and Buckingham himself stepped forward to guide the King's hand.

Kenelm heard the congratulations of the Court afterwards as if in a dream; he was the same as he had always been, and was glad enough to ride back towards the south, knowing Bristol lay already in the Tower by Buckingham's enmity and would shortly be released under house-arrest at his great house of Sherborne in Dorset, the same to which Venetia had been taken, that had once belonged to Sir Walter Raleigh and had been given to Somerset of disgraceful memory, then to John.

As Kenelm rode on his way, he espied a gilded carriage, making its way slowly along the road from town. Inside was a beautiful woman with an oval face and hazel eyes, and bright hair in ringlets about her shoulders.

It was Venetia. And he loved her as much as ever.

The King was not well, and had taken to his bed; the comfort brought by the return of his Steenie and Baby Charles, as he perpetually called his son, had cheered him for the time being; but he was sensible of the rebuff from Spain, it had all been costly as well as humiliating, and also his daughter's plight still troubled James; she was poor, living with her husband and family in Holland; a mercy perhaps that his dearest bedfellow had died before it all happened. He himself had tried to work for peace, and indeed there had been no war, on the whole; the Spanish one had ended the year after he came to the throne. A memory of long-dead Salisbury's face came to the sick man, restless on his pillows. The hunchback could no doubt die easy after having made that peace. In fact, what had anyone on their conscience, in particular himself? He shut out the memory of the tortured dead, of Somerset and his wife in the Tower, of Bristol lately sent there also to placate Buckingham.

Steenie was becoming exorbitant in his demands. Could he be trusted? Could he? An old weak man lying in his bed would be an easy target for . . . what? James narrowed his hooded eyelids to where the tall long-legged splendid figure waited now, always near him, never leaving him alone. Alone. Had he not been so all his life, not even remembering his own mother, brought up to hate her, to suffer even her execution in his determined, stubborn, secret bid for the English crown? But he had won that, and his warlike handsome ancestors had not; he, weak-legged timid ridiculed James Stuart, had won. But now Steenie . . .

The King called out faintly for Baby Charles to come. The small patient figure came, and knelt beside his father.

"What would Your Majesty?" Not expected to live, this one had been, James remembered; yet Charles would gain the crown, and glorious Henry Frederick, who would have worn it superbly, was dead and rotten. He himself and Henry had not seen eye to eye and there had been rumours that he, the young Prince's own father, had poisoned him. Poison. It was always there, in his mind, like the shining of swords, like gunpowder, to be feared. Steenie . . . he and Baby Charles were firm friends now where once they had been enemies. The new reign would start strongly, with the two friends together, and the old man who had been like a father to them both dead, and not regretted.

James turned his grey head towards his son. "Be advised," he said clearly. "When I am dead, dinna give all things into the hands of ane man; spread your favours."

"Sire, you are not dead but alive, and hopefully will grow better of this sickness. But as you have said it, I wanted to ask you to let me appoint Sir Kenelm Digby a councillor."

"Digby . . . his father was a plotter . . . he is a Papist."

"But hath many friends in the Church of England. He is a man of wise parts and much learning, of a fascinating kind. You yourself would delight in his talk."

"I will never know delight again." Had he ever known it? Long ago there had been the fair beauty of young Robin Carr, lying injured after a tourney; James had gone to the boy often until Carr's broken leg had healed, and then had loved him. And long ago he had crossed the stormy seas to Norway to find his Danish bride, and had maybe loved her too, for a while. And Steenie . . .

"Have your friends on your council," he whispered. "I am not well. As to your marriage . . . you must marry, despite Spain . . ."

"The youngest daughter of Henri IV is marriageable and they regard my suit with favour." Charles spoke coldly. He remembered seeing young Henrietta Maria dancing at the Louvre when he and Steenie were in disguise there as Tom and

John Smith, travelling through France towards Spain. He could not remember her face, only the small thin young figure moving correctly in the dance.

"She will be a Papist," murmured the King. "They made her father say Paris was worth a Mass. He was a bonny fighter when he was a Protestant."

"And a good King later. Maybe we will make children, the French princess and I, who will have his qualities."

"Then they will be grand lechers." The dying face smiled, showing the dribbled lines at the corners of the mouth where the too-big tongue had let out saliva constantly. "Take my hand, Baby Charles," the King whispered. "I do not feel mysel' today."

"Shall I fetch Steenie to you? He is here, and would serve you gladly."

"No, not him . . . not Steenie . . ."

The King died soon, and Charles I was King. Most powerful in the land now would be, as formerly, Buckingham. A rumour started that he had poisoned the dead King, who had been losing trust in him. The funeral was magnificent, with a wax likeness of James lying stiffly in

Westminster Abbey for seven days, then raised to its feet to denote the monarch's undoubted passing into Heaven. By that time the commissioners for the French marriage proposal were chosen and sent off, and among them, beside Buckingham himself, rode Kenelm Digby.

He had not thought he would be able to join the commission; he was too poor, having spent what he had in Spain. They all had; even Bristol had had to pay his own fare back home by selling his silver plate, and little good that had done him where he lay now in the Tower. Buckingham was jealous, that was it; soon, and carefully, the faithful servant would be freed if his friends continued to feel the way.

But Kenelm could not be careful. He stood in a certain room where two plain women sat in the background with their sewing, and the most beautiful object in the world before his eyes. He had lost no time in visiting Venetia and had found her unchanged despite all they said; unchanged, and most lovable.

"I hear you are going to France," he

heard her say. Islip had been dismissed long ago, but Venetia's friends still brought her the Court gossip although she no longer appeared there.

"Alas, I doubt me I cannot." He let dejection sound in his voice; after all, how could he afford even to worship this creature, used to the best as she was in everything? He could bring her no gift except his love.

"Hear me—" he had begun, but Venetia put one of her slender hands on his sleeve, another against his lips.

"Have no fear," she said. "You shall go to France."

"Venetia, I may not go! What sort of figure would I cut?" The question brought him down, disagreeably, to solid earth: it would have been better merely to stay and adore her, not talk about money.

After he had gone Venetia called for her jewel-box. She owed Kenelm as much; he still lived, and still loved her; it was a solace to find one who did. Dorset had taken the children into care, and had made her an annuity; he had acted generously after his way, no doubt. But Kenelm; he had a title now. She beckoned to one of the maids. She kept the women always about her these days, so that her reputation, if it could be white by now, should be so again.

"Take this to the Scots jeweller. See what he will give you for them. I want a good price." She knew of the man, who had come south with King James in 1603 and since then had made his fortune in London; they said the Queen had died owing him thousands of pounds. Venetia could not recall his name. The woman would know.

Later, Venetia wrote a note to Kenelm.

Pray you come to me. I have the wherewithal to take you to France, comfortably.

He could never be grateful enough. Before, he had loved her beauty and her way of speech; now he could love her generous soul. He kissed her hands time and again, for once speechless with gratitude. "For you to do this for me! I am your slave." That he had been always; Venetia smiled, her eyes lighting up with more of happiness than she had felt for a long time. It was good to have Kenelm with her again. She had always been very fond of him. And to establish his credit with the new French Queen would do no harm. The newly made Duke of Buckingham, Lord Warden of the Cinque Ports, should not have it all his own way; they said he had already spent far more than was needed on more jewellery, suits of clothes, and plumed hats to ride into Paris, as though he had been the bridegroom.

Kenelm stood alone in the room by the curtained bed. The servants had led him in and left him there, being accustomed by now to his presence in the house. No doubt they thought of him as the successor to Dorset.

Saddened by that, he gently drew the bed-curtains and stood looking down on Venetia's sleeping face. Her beauty was without stain; so perfect a thing, he thought, must be rare indeed; and he had even seen Europe's most beautiful woman, the Queen of France, Anne of Austria, with whom Buckingham had fallen madly in love on the venture in Paris.

Anne had had a jutting Hapsburg lip, which titillated her admirers; and brown hair, not unlike Venetia's. The latter lay loose on her white shoulders now, and if he would he could pick up a lock of it and kiss it, and lay it back again, and she— But he did not want to wake her, it was too great a happiness to be able to watch her when she was unaware of him, defenceless against any movement he might make. But he would make none, of that kind. Dorset had acted differently.

He knew swift anger at the thought, again so soon, of Dorset. At the Court of France they had thought him, Digby, moody and silent; it had been because he knew well enough that he was there because of Venetia's money, perhaps in that case even Dorset's. What honourable man would have accepted such generosity without making amends? What must he do? He knew very well; he must brave his mother's wrath and marry Venetia. When she should awake, perhaps he would tell her; perhaps; or prolong this moment of delight?

Her lips were coral, lightly parted to show small white teeth. The lashes on her cheek were long, silken and dark, the cheeks themselves slightly flushed with sleep. He could imagine no better fate than to see her thus, all parts of her, daily, nightly. From the beginning she had been his, should have remained his, never that other's. But she had never loved Dorset. He was sure of it. If it had not been for the rumour of his own death she would have remained faithful.

In any event, what were bodies except the outward shell of the soul? Had her soul changed, except to show generosity? And he should be the last to question it, he who had taken the bright tress of her hair at last and thrown it on the fire. And the vision of her the Brahman showed him had been desolate with grief.

He removed his shoes and, moving carefully not to wake her, slid between the sheets, lying at last by her, doing no more than enjoy her near presence; her sweet breath came to him, and he noted the curve of her lips, which was unlike any other woman's he knew of, so gently pleasing was it. He lay there till she wakened; stirring awake, aware already that there was something amiss, turning with a shock to see him lying there, even ready to oust him, the nearness of his great warm body perturbing her, but he seized her and began to kiss her. At first she struggled, then submitted to it; he told her clearly that he would not wrong her, that she was safe with him.

"Let me go at once. You are worse than Mr. Clerk." That personage was a gentleman of the bedchamber to the King, and had long desired Venetia, so much so that he had begged Kenelm to intercede for him. But thoughts of that were far away now. Kenelm drew his fingers through the beautiful hair, revelling in its warmth and softness. She drew away, the hair half veiling her face. "How can I persuade you that my affection hath neither heat nor cold, but is most constant?" he asked her. Venetia blushed deeply.

"How can I endure such an affection? Even my portrait is with Lord Dorset still. No woman of honour would have left it with him, and now I cannot obtain it."

"I will retrieve it for you. I will fight him if I need." He was filled with confidence, remembering the success of his brawl in Spain. He would put Dorset back where he belonged, in the shades! He kissed her again, this time on the lips, and when she begged him to stop said suddenly: "Sing to me, Venetia. I want to hear your voice."

Astoundingly, she obeyed; a fragile song about honour and love's pure flame. He left her, determined to seek out Dorset and obtain the portrait to return to her. He still turned over in his mind the notion of marrying her; that should be done when he had retrieved what he had promised.

He challenged Dorset, and although at first his challenge was accepted, my lord withdrew later out of caution, and returned the portrait to Kenelm. This was a triumph, and he hastened to restore it to Venetia; at the end, taking both her hands, he exclaimed: "Now you belong to none but me."

Mr. Clerk, and all the others, were forgotten. But to his chagrin she refused his proposal of marriage. He flung off, angry because she had said he had had no faith in her, that time. How could it have been helped, when the false rumour of his death had not been contradicted? He pleaded with her that he had written, but that the letter could not have reached her, and gradually she began to see reason; gradually realized that his love for her was a part of his life, and would not alter now.

Kenelm had expected some embarrassment when he went in Buckingham's train to Paris, if he should again meet the Queen Dowager of France, Marie de Médicis. Last time he had seen her had been on a bed, which he had forcefully refused to share: and the report of his death would now be confounded by the fact that he was very much alive, and in the company. But Queen Marie was as powerless now as Queen Anne, both women being out of favour with son and husband. When Buckingham tried to make love to Anne of Austria at last in a secluded garden she cried out, the attendants came running, and there was great scandal; but King Charles's marriage was by then made in any case and the little French princess was safely brought to England, where the common people could not pronounce the name of Henriette and so called her Queen

Mary. It was evident from the beginning that, despite marriage, scandal and everything else, Buckingham still ruled the King, to the new Queen's great resentment.

Kenelm knew most of it, but was too greatly taken up with Venetia to pay any heed. At times they quarrelled and at others were reconciled, and once again he had to challenge a young man to a duel on her behalf, and once again have it refused, such was his size and known prowess. The matter had sprung from a meeting on the river, when Kenelm and his friends in one boat espied Venetia and other young women in another, veiled against the hot day, while the willow branches trailed among them purling the water agreeably. It was all resolved in the end, but not before Bristol had heard of it even at Sherborne. He sent for Kenelm, to advise him like a father, as he hoped. He was fond of the young man, and also grateful; Kenelm had bearded old King James in person on his behalf, whether or not this was the reason for a lighter form of imprisonment. Bristol kept his ear to the ground where he was, and knew, or seemed to know, everything that happened at Court, which had grown elegant and correct if not prudish; the new King was different from the old.

"They say you have forsaken all pursuit of knowledge in your passion for this young woman," Bristol told him, not mincing matters; they sat in the very garden at Sherborne whence Venetia had once made her nocturnal escape. The arbour on the little hill was still there, but the vine had withered.

"I love her because she is she and I am I," said Kenelm at last, after much argument. It was true that he could think of nothing but Venetia. His round eyes regarded his kinsman with some caution. Should he unburden himself further? Surely Bristol, with his diplomatic expertise, could keep a secret?

"Sir," he said, "tell none, but Venetia and I are married these four months."

He did not add that Venetia was four months gone with child. Bristol shook his head gravely. "It will," he said, "be a great grief to your mother. She had hoped for greater things from you."

Indeed the remembrance of Mary Digby

was chiefly the reason for the marriage's having been kept secret. Kenelm could not think how in the world he was to break the news at Gothurst. Yet it would have to be done sooner or later, when the child should come. He tried to picture the child and could not. It would, he assured himself, be beautiful as an angel, like its mother. But his mind stayed empty.

That summer of 1625 there was plague in the slums of the city, as happened every so often; but this was a bad year, and the Court left London. In the unspeakable conditions behind St. Margaret's and in Holborn, priests worked tirelessly to bring aid to the victims and, if necessary, the viaticum. It was easier for them to come and go now there was a Catholic Queen, for though Henrietta had caused ill feeling by refusing to be crowned in the Church of England rite, there was relief meantime for Catholics everywhere, and in fact had been since the opening of the earlier marriage negotiations with Spain.

Kenelm escorted Venetia out to Enston

Abbey and they travelled by coach, with the windows closed despite the heat. The city's streets were silent except for the sound of wheels as one equipage after another trailed out to the Oxford road. Behind closed doors, ragged gaunt folk watched other gaunt folk die; and the doors themselves were marked with red crosses, if there was a door; otherwise, victims lay in the street. Venetia stared ahead of her in silence; Kenelm brought to mind the new Queen's bounty and how he had sent one of his servants to give it, and something from himself, to the ministering priests. Other than that he had done little for his faith over the years, growing lax as some others had done; he told himself he was no worse than they. In the north, in Lancashire, it was different; so one had heard. But he was here, in London.

He left Venetia at her father's house at last and himself rode to Gothurst to see his mother. He found Mary rigidly at prayer, which made up most of her days now; the soul of his father would be well assoiled, Kenelm thought; and tried to banish gloom from his own thoughts, but dared not tell her yet of his marriage. The place was the same; the lily pond shone in the sun, the maze wound darkly, the oak avenue shaded all comers. Johnny was at home, but there was not enough confidence between the brothers for Kenelm to unburden himself as he had done to Bristol. Besides, Johnny himself was a potential rival; their mother was free to leave the inheritance to the younger son if she should cut out Kenelm. He recognized cowardice, even greed, in himself, but would do nothing. He dared not become penniless when his child was about to be born, as it proved, in Shropshire; Venetia travelled there to visit her solitary father, who knew nothing of her marriage either. It said much for the fashions the new Queen had brought that a woman's condition could be hidden till the eighth month, by reason of the full skirts, the pointed bodices beneath a wide collar. Venetia looked beautiful still; but when did she not look so?

He was still at Gothurst, intent on chemical experiments, when word came suddenly: he left the flasks by the cooling fire, and rode north at speed. He was frantic with anxiety; Venetia had been out riding, and had fallen, was bruised, and had sent for him. Surely the child would be hurt, perhaps born dead! He still found that he could hardly think of the child; and now, in her absence, could instead centre his thoughts on Venetia in the old way, as someone in danger, glorious and unattainable. The fact that he had attained her, that they had lived together for months as man and wife, no doubt rousing much gossip, did not seem real.

When he flung himself at last into the hall at Tonge, leaving his lathered horse with the grooms, he was led by a maid-servant straight to Venetia's chamber. There was no sign of old Sir Edward and no doubt he was among his books. Kenelm entered the room fearfully; then gave a shout of joy. She was there, poised and beautiful, on the pillows, freshly combed and washed; and in her arm a small quiet head showed among swaddlings. He went and knelt to her and their son. "What befell?" he heard himself ask hoarsely. It had not yet been time for the birth; he had expected news of a miscarriage, of worse, perhaps Venetia's very death. But she was alive, and beautiful.

"What befell? *I* had a fall from the saddle, and *he* was born among my skirts, and my father himself, who was with me, knows nothing." She began to laugh; they both began to laugh; Kenelm kissed his son. He was aware of a tenderness creeping up within him that he had never before known; he had never seen the child begotten by him long ago on the Marchesa; this was his first true son. He imitated the gesture of new fathers worldwide and proffered his finger to the baby to grasp. "Do not play with him too much yet," Venetia said. "He needs sleep, to gather strength."

It was the only reference she made to the sudden pain of the birth, and her only aid, from the small frightened maid-servant; and without clearly knowing why, he was grateful. He made ready to convey his respects to Sir Edward Stanley, who if he thought about it at all must surely wonder why a young man was so suddenly in his house. But the old scholar received him kindly if absently, his spectacles sliding down his nose towards a volume of Baronius he was busied with. He bade Kenelm stay as long as he chose; there was no such enmity towards Mary Digby's son as Mary still felt for himself, and it was good, as he said, for Venetia to have young friends: it was quiet here in the country, and Kenelm might stay for as long as it pleased him.

Kenelm stayed as long as he might, then rode back to London, leaving Venetia with a further pledge of his love, his son with many kisses.

Digby, in those early years of his secret marriage, had already earned glowing opinions for the working of his Powder of Sympathy whose prescription he had got from the Carmelite monk in Italy. An acquaintance who had been with him in Spain, one James Howell, injured his hand in trying to prevent a duel between friends, and although the friends called off the duel at once and rushed to his assistance, the hand was deeply wounded front and back. The friends bound it up with a garter and surgeons put a plaster on it later, but it continued in great heat and was very painful. "They say it may come to a gangrene," said Howell dolefully to Kenelm when he met him one day on a riverside walk, well bandaged. Kenelm looked at the hand, besought Howell to make use of his own services, and availed himself of the bloodstained garter to sink in a basin of water mixed with the vitriolic powder. Immediately Howell reported himself eased, as though a wet napkin had been placed over the wounds. Kenelm then took the garter out of the solution and set it before the fire to dry, and almost at once there was a knocking on the door and Howell's servant entered, saying his master's heat and agony had grown again as great as ever.

Kenelm put the garter back in the cool solution. "Go back to your master, who will be eased by now," he said to the servant. "Do not come back if all is well."

All was indeed well, whether by means of the Powder of Sympathy or by washing off the effects of the surgeons' plasters, would never be known, but Kenelm was pleased. He had begun to feel himself increasingly useless despite his constant experiments and writings, and here, perhaps, was a proof that it was not so.

King James himself had taken an interest in the Powder, and promised on having received its secret to reveal this to no one, and to prepare it always with his own hands; but of course he told Buckingham, and Buckingham told the world. One way or another, Kenelm and the Powder grew famous.

He was becoming famous also, however, for what the world still saw as his liaison with Venetia. Among the first to question him openly about it was one who had a right to do so, for Bristol had been good to him. He came upon Kenelm cooking, and Kenelm left the ingredients in the mortar and pestle where he had been pounding them, and came to his kinsman, wiping his hands.

"I am honoured by my lord's visit," he said a little uneasily. Bristol did not smile. "Kenelm, there is much said against you. I do not mince my words." He cast a glance of some scorn at the shelled eggs and herbs; he did not consider such matters a man's occupation. Kenelm was flushed from the heat of the fire in his rooms; he looked at the floor.

"Look into your own mind a little," said Bristol, stroking his glove. "You used to make much of your studies; what good are they to you now? What have you done to serve the King and forward your own cause? You used to have zeal and vigour for everything you did, now—" He broke off, and Kenelm knew what he had left unsaid; an idle wencher, lover of a woman of no reputation, pleasing himself and no other. He thought of Venetia and their child, and his heart was torn in him; but he could not make the marriage public yet.

"A marriage with Venetia Stanley will do nothing to advance your state," said Bristol, frowning, as though he had read Kenelm's mind. "Your mother's estate may well be left away from you if she is displeased; where would that leave you? Let not the world say that all your learning and understanding and vigour cannot defend you from the snares of beauty."

"I do wish myself out of the world," muttered Kenelm. "No exterior thing is worth the exchanging of one's leisure." He was ashamed of the words as soon as he had uttered them, and flung up his head. "I am confident that *her* life will belie any

230

rumour that may have been spread abroad by tattle and believed by those who take their opinions upon trust."

There was a knock at the door; it was Lord Bristol's lawyer, come after him to discuss an urgent matter of business, which called him away for the time. But Kenelm returned to his ruined dish with the resolve growing in him that he must do two things; he must somehow let the world know that his marriage to Venetia was honourable, and also he must carry out some brave action which would earn him recognition from the King. Others had done it; Sir Walter Raleigh had sailed to El Dorado. It was a mournful reminder; on return, without any gold, Raleigh had had his head cut off. But perhaps all such ventures would not be unlucky.

Venetia was, predictably, with child again. Having heard to his indignation that the Court believed she was his mistress as she had been Sackville's, Kenelm decided that the time had come to break the news of his marriage to his mother, at least. It was a risk; she might disinherit him; but it must be taken. He took young Kenelm, now two years old, with his nurse, and rode to Gothurst beside the coach. "Keep him safe," Venetia had begged, but would not come herself; she feared Mary Digby no little, and was sick in the mornings besides. Kenelm would never have admitted to himself that the glory of his vision of Venetia would hardly withstand the rub of day to day; close-stools, menstrual periods, linen to be washed, oneself to be washed, the inconvenience of pregnancy and its concealment meantime. He made his mind dwell on other things, riding in the fresh air, how forward and handsome his son was. Surely his mother would never disown such an heir!

He was right; Mary Digby burst into tears. "He is the image of your father," she declared, hardly listened to the news of the marriage, and took the child in her arms, regarding him hungrily. Young Kenelm, who was of a placid and agreeable disposition, allowed himself to be kissed. Later Mary told her son that she had heard rumours of his marriage, from Lady Horsey and others who seemed to hear all news before it reached Court, as is the way with old dames.

"I did not think you would live sinfully with her for so long a time," she said. "It is maybe for the best." Then her gaze returned to her grandson, of whom she could never see enough; he had saved the day, but Mary never would meet her son's wife. Digby kept his family and his marriage strictly apart, treating the latter almost as a diplomatic question; he would ride to Gothurst at times alone, at other times with the nurse and young Kenelm, who grew prodigiously. Meantime, Digby's conscience attacked him from another direction: he must perform that noble deed to serve the King, perhaps thereby recapturing, in his own mind, the glory of morning in his absent love.

He went to Charles, accordingly. The King had grown in presence since his father's death; a small pointed beard, as was fashionable, had given effect to his pale features, and as always he showed taste in his manners and in the elegance of his attire. His marriage was not yet too happy; he himself was still ruled by Buckingham, and the young Queen resented it fiercely. A son had been born to her, and had died the same day. That was unfortunate; but the Court was already different from that of the disgraceful Somersets and the favoured pretty boys of old King James. Courtiers were discreet and mannerly, in public at least; and the Queen practised her religion freely and had even ordered an altarpiece by Peter Paul Rubens to be set up in her chapel at Somerset House.

5

"SIRE, I am anxious to put my sword and my person at your service."

Charles smiled a little, regarding the large eager figure before him. Kenelm was flamboyantly dressed, in a high lace collar and a coat of wine-coloured velvet laced with silver. His tapering hands gestured as they always did, accompanying his talk. Now he placed the right hand over his heart.

"I would beg the favour of letters of marque in order that I may take to sea in Your Majesty's cause."

Charles, who was rarely stirred to laughter, felt an uprush of affection for this big bumbling man. Digby was loyal, he was certain; but so had Buckingham been, yet Steenie's late disastrous attack on the Île de Rhé had brought nothing but dishonour to England, and to oneself. To allow courtiers free passage and command on the high seas was almost certainly to court unpopularity abroad, perhaps even danger at home. Yet Charles was anxious that England should have a navy. He hesitated, trying to control his stammering tongue. Before he could speak, Digby bubbled into talk again. "Sire, it can be, once more, as it was in the days of Drake and Walter Raleigh. I would use all endeavour to bring home goods and treasure to Your Majesties both. There is a man named Ward who hath achieved as much from nothing, less than I am; permit me to show my loyalty in such a way."

"You would have no aid at sea. All nations there are against England, even for those few among us who seek not war or treasure, but antique works of art. It would p-please me if you brought those." The young King was already showing himself an enlightened collector of Grecian marbles and of paintings, the latter mostly from France and Flanders.

"Those, too, I will bring," promised Kenelm. In his present mood of elation he could do anything; if only—he dared admit it—he could be free of home!

Charles gave permission, but there was delay, and Kenelm had to run the gauntlet between a sobbing Venetia at home and his enemy, or rather Bristol's, at Court; the Duke of Buckingham, the Lord High Admiral himself. In the end the letters of marque had to be acquired through him. Kenelm detested him by now as many did, but downed his dislike of the arrogant dark head with its frame of jewels and lace. Much damage had been done to Lord Bristol by the Duke's tongue; that Kenelm could not forgive, and it was probable that my lord Duke by now distrusted all of the name of Digby.

"And leave your fair Venetia?" drawled Buckingham. Kenelm flushed. Although his mother now knew of the marriage, others did not; and his pride forbade him to say so straight out to the King's favourite. To leave Venetia was in truth one aim; he could think of her delightfully when he did not have to endure the fusses of everyday. "I will leave those I love for the King's service, as any honest man must do," he retorted hotly.

"You attribute many things to honest men; I believe you are even known to have said that an attentive husband may make a good wife out of a brothel-keeper."

"Your Grace flatters me by recalling such things," said Digby through his teeth. "It is the truth, no more. Shall a clear stream be sullied by stirring up mud?"

Buckingham, who should have known, said nothing. By the end, Kenelm had his permission to set sail and to disrupt, if he might, the trade in French silks with Portugal and Spain. He went home with the news, and Venetia shed a few tears; would he leave her so? How had she offended him? But by the end she was almost relieved not to have his large, earnest presence about her during the weary days of waiting while the child grew heavy in her. Men always gave one a child, then went off on their own affairs.

Last of all he said farewell to Bristol, who had done much to implant in him the desire to serve the King. My lord, in his own house where Kenelm had ordered the coach to come for Dover, greeted him gravely. He asked him directly of his reported marriage, and Kenelm was hard put to it to answer; he was not ready to make the marriage to Venetia public yet;

238

it should be done some day, some day soon, when he had reason; but not yet. So he regarded his kinsman with some dismay. "Your great familiarity with her makes men say you are married, and yet there is no word from you," Bristol told him frankly. He laid a hand on the young man's sleeve. Kenelm dropped his gaze, then suddenly raised it to meet the Earl's candid eyes.

"I am married," he said. "I had not thought to make it known, for many reasons."

Bristol nodded. "Your position is delicate," he said. "I myself will look to your wife, while you are away, and will use her with all honour."

Tears rose to Kenelm's eyes. "I have much to thank you for," he said. "You raised me from being the son of an attainted rebel to a position which is something esteemed, if not yet enough."

"Your own talents embellish your fair name," smiled Bristol. He heard Kenelm make the kind of speech expected of him; he would go to seek glory, to serve the King, if necessary to die a glorious death for England. "There is one thing more, and it is secret," Bristol told him. "The King wants you to treat for peace, if you may, with the leader of the Barbary pirates, the Bassa of Algiers. There are more than two hundred Englishmen held in their gaols; with a trifle of goodwill they might be set free."

"I will essay it." He would have done battle with armies, navies; he must burnish his reputation, partly for Venetia's sake, partly for his own. Young Kenelm should not have the fouled start he himself had had to make in life; he should be proud of his father even were he to remain only a memory.

The coach rumbled off, and the last sight of Bristol Kenelm had was of the latter's farewell from the steps of his house; Kenelm kept his head turned till the corner of the street, when the fine raised hand in its deep lace cuff could be seen no longer. Excitement rose in him; the adventure was begun!

Soon he saw the Downs, and the unending sea, with his ships rocking bravely on its glitter; it was a fine day. He prayed the wind would serve, and turned smiling to Sir Edward Stradling, the

Welshman who would serve under him, who had joined the coach.

"Here is a messenger," said Sir Edward as they made ready to embark. The man's horse was foam-flecked; he thrust a letter into Kenelm's hand, grinning broadly.

Kenelm fumbled with the folded paper, finally tore it open; it was from home. Venetia had given birth safely to a second fine son. Joy rose in him and he spoke loudly, hoping the world might hear.

"You may tell my wife to keep silence no longer concerning our marriage." He heard his voice loud in the clear day. He had to say it; it was the least he could do for his sons' mother.

It took a fortnight of waiting for the wind to be favourable. Kenelm passed his time in reading, writing, striding the decks of his own ship the *Eagle*, four hundred tons afloat; the two smaller, the *Elizabeth* and the *George*, waited at anchor. Delay of this kind taxed Kenelm's patience; he liked quick results in anything, an experiment, a potion, a love affair. While the thought of adventure at sea was still fresh he wanted to be up and doing, wielding his sword and firing his guns, not idling here in his cabin.

But the wind changed; he felt it freshening on his face at last from the northeast. It was cold. "Let down sail!" he roared. "The wind is with us!"

The canvas filled, bellying out in the bitter January breeze; as the *Eagle* drew out from the shore, Kenelm saw the figures of the small crowd which had gathered to watch, attracted by their cries and orders, grow smaller; white cliffs merged with distant downs, and the *Eagle* was under way. He thought of little else for some hours, then remembered the few lines he had been able to scrawl to Venetia, again bidding her make their marriage public at last. There must be no more sneers from Buckingham and his like. By God, he would do better for the King than that popinjay had done in France! The good north-easter filling the sails filled his lungs also, and he breathed deeply of the cold sparkling air. The shores of England were almost out of vision; soon they would sight France. He stood by the helm, watching the sliding green water on which there already fell a few flakes of snow. It was true; he, Digby, was in command, and at sea. He would do wondrous things; the fact that he was not yet certain what they might be made it the more venturesome. He saluted the Vice-Admiral, behind him in the *Elizabeth.* He, Admiral of the King's ships, bound for the Mediterranean! He, Kenelm Digby, the son of . . .

But his mind faltered as he remembered his father, and he made himself busy about the helm and the deck, afterwards giving place to his second-in-command, and making for his cabin to sleep as night fell. The even progress of the ship lulled him and soon, he slept.

They stopped a Fleming three days later, but she had been already pillaged by another Englishman and was allowed to proceed, her flat-faced crew murmuring and sullen. Next day they chased a Frenchman but did not catch up fast enough; and made stern chase two days later of five Dutch vessels, who also got away. Kenelm's temper grew short as he kept his log-book; was this to be all his reward, and was he to take back to the King nothing but a tale of winds?

One of the crew came up to him. "Sir, there is a leak in the powder-room." Already the wind was freshening to a storm, and later it continued, rocking them unhappily so that water slapped the sides. They stopped the leak, and had care to the ship, and to the rest following behind; but the gale blew for three days, and as it steadied a great ship loomed up out of the evening, and made ready to fight. Kenelm came on deck, and gave orders to man the guns; but the ship changed its mind and made off, leaving him foolish. They chased the great ship for some hours, but could not catch or name her. Next day they sighted Portugal, having weathered the bay; that was something. Cape St. Vincent passed astern, almost in calm; and soon, rising out of the yellow dawn, they saw at last a strange wild range of hills upthrusting black against the sky; the coast of High Barbary.

"We must attempt the Strait by night, sir, to baffle the Spaniard."

"Well, then, do so." He was beguiled

by the sudden calm; in this wild place he stared out to sea to the south, and again back to the Spanish coast, half regretful that he could not make his mark there; but nowadays, at least outwardly, there was amity with Spain. So they passed the Rock by night, and by early morning had entered into the most ancient sea in the world, with its legendary waters embracing Spain and Africa and further lands still out of sight. Kenelm stood on deck and let the sun warm him, glad at heart after the sour delays and useless pursuits they had had further north. He felt a sensation of power come; it tingled from the tips of his fingers to his very sword, hanging by him; the hairs of his head seemed alive with it, his big body tensed, his mind calm.

But at first there was nothing to attack but a Hamburg ship, which fired across their bows. At last Kenelm could tell his crew to open flint-locks, fire the powder, hear the cannon roar, see the turbid water splash and sputter, hear the cries of men, urging one another on in the kind of friendly rivalry that still obtained in any war. In the *Elizabeth* and the *George* Stradling had given orders to fire, and the smoke rose all about them, blinding them and carried off by no wind.

"They will take our masts," he said at last, through the uproar. "They will have little on board but wine and fruit. We must save our strength for greater things. It is best to withdraw."

When the smoke cleared, the ship was out of sight. The men seemed laggard and dejected. Kenelm wished that he might soon have a worthwhile victory.

To the Right Honourable the Earl of Bristol, at his house in London. This day the first of February, 1628.

My very good Lord and deare Cousin,
    After my last there is little more news but of sickness. 16 of the crew this afternoon fell down, which hath left us very short in the meantime. None the less we made ready to fight a sayle descried, and fitting herself for fight, but turned out to be an Englishman; all do run from us except they. But I never yett met with any English, were they never so little and contemptible vessels, but they steyed for us and made readie for fight.

Yesterday also midday, we chased 2 sayles, and before dark fetched 'em up. They were Flemish, and the crew was drunk. I sent men abord, then more, to master them, but mine were verie disorderly and pillaged their wooden chests and clothes. They much complained to me, and I punished those I should. I have yet myself to search the ships, and am in some haste to doe so, so will close with my much duty.

He searched the Flemings amongst the persistent grumbling of both sides, checked the bills of lading, and licensed them doubtfully; he had the feeling that all was not as he saw it. A flutter of papers had caught his eyes, falling into the sea. But it was by then growing dark, and he went back on board his *Eagle*.

As night fell, he set the compass and soon descried seven sail. They were small ships, but grazed him at last with a broadside astern, and made off. He gave orders to fire; this was done, and returned with a great clamour of broadsides. Through the smoke and growing blackness Kenelm made out the single figure of their commander, and drew on till within pistol reach, when he shot close and so did the other. Stradling in the *George* was doing likewise, and their shot peppered the sea. At last the other commander hailed Digby, and said his name was Horn. Silence fell, the guns no longer sounding; the warm Mediterranean night waited, and already, at the prows, lanterns were lit.

"I order you to fall amain," called Digby, "for the King of England." His voice rang out confidently; were they not victorious? "Come aboard," yelled the other, and when Kenelm made a move to go across, raked him with gunfire; he was not hit. *I then gave over all other discourse but of my great gunnes, which we played so well that by nine of the clocke hee begun to fall off from us with his consortes and wee heard them make lamentable cryes.* There were not men enough left to use the great guns; the sickness was spreading, as though a curse were on the ship. With fifty sick, there were perhaps a further thirty left who could fight and man her. He had to let the enemy go: but he was somewhat comforted, for a shot had passed through his own cabin, destroying most of it, another near his head, instead holing the sails, and one man had lost an arm on their side, another an ear. All this was evident and would grow in the telling; but the sickness also grew.

It was a curious sickness; despite his mortification he could not help but be interested in the symptoms. There were headaches and stomach-ache; the blood in the veins he thought was putrefied, for some tried to suck their own and could not. There was the smell of blood and vomit on deck and in the hold, yet the men lingered on, able to keep down nothing, not even the brackish water he had taken on at their last port. Help seemed in itself to kill the men quickly; seeing the bodies lie about and nobody but himself with the strength to heave them overboard, Kenelm gave orders that no further aid should be given; that way there was a chance of life. The hammocks below deck grew filled with stinking bodies, and those who had gone down to rob them often died by their sides, lying still. The Powder of Sympathy was far away.

Others went mad. They cried out for oranges, and there were none to be had, then in search of what they thought in despair was coolness they would writhe out of the portholes or fling themselves from the decks into the sea, which they saw as grass. Digby was met within a day or two by the chief officers from all three ships, none of whom had themselves succumbed; the thought passed his mind that maybe the food issued to crews caused it, the ship's biscuit and beef by now grown black, and cheese grown mouldy. But he heard with dismay what the rest had to tell him; they begged him to return to England.

Kenelm grew pale beneath the tan the sun had brought. "We are so far now on our way it would be further to return home than to pursue our goal."

"Sir, it is dead calm."

The sea brooded; was it his fancy that it smiled at his misfortunes, he the brash newcome adventurer, the pillager? "We must take heed to the men," was all he would say, and continued to do his best for them, for the most of ten days; by the end of that, those who were to die were dead, and thrown overboard. The weather was strange; once they even had a hail-storm, but never a favourable wind. The sick men raised their faces to the cold rain when it came, mouths agape; they sucked the wet from their sweat-sodden clothes, licked at the decks and spars. By the end the fever left them; by the end, which seemed an eternity, the ship resumed her course; and at last they came within sight of a great bay with square-rigged ships already in building, for these saved the weight of ship's biscuit and oarsmen in galleys; the galleys of the sea-wolves, the pirates of Algiers. This was where he, Digby, was to treat for peace.

The English consul, a Mr. Friswell, clad in drab linen against the heat, greeted Kenelm and the officers and took them to his flat-topped house, white in the sun's glare and with date-palms somehow straggling above the surrounding dust. Kenelm stared with thankfulness at the fruit; the sick men could be fed that and the oranges they had craved, for there was a market throwing black shadows and promising lemons and wine and leather shoes with the points upturned; he had seen them as he passed by. There had been delay in permission to land, and Friswell was still flushed with his efforts. Kenelm said to him: "Had I stayed forty-eight hours longer, there would not have been men enough to sail my ship."

The consul stared at the eccentric English admiral, whose hair and beard had grown long as though he were a savage; the rest were in like case, hardly resembling the dapper gentlemen who had set out from Dover. Friswell said nothing, however, and gave them wine. It would depend on this odd Englishman, he decided, whether or not the Bassa would favour him; after all, he might or might not. Friswell himself had barely escaped being burned alive by the Bassa's order some weeks since, so one never knew. Now, all seemed peace.

The Earl of Bristol called on Venetia and found her seated languidly by the fire, while a little old man read verses to her. She rose to her feet, smiled at Ben Jonson, and came to greet her husband's kinsman. Jonson took his cue and left, while Venetia pressed him warmly to return soon; she had this kindness which made her beloved of many humble folk, while the proud ignored her.

Bristol seated himself at her invitation after kissing the exquisite hands; they were cool and scented. She wore a velvet gown of a crimson colour, for the weather was cold, and over her shoulders a small fur cape nestled against the bitter draughts from the window. She seemed unchanged from any other time he had ever seen her; her beauty was flowerlike and she had not aged or thickened with the births. He asked for her children, young Kenelm and the other, the new John; as for the rest by Dorset, as he was now since his brother's death. No doubt they were in the country with their nurse. He was uncertain whether or not Kenelm entertained them; doubtless their father looked after them.

"My son is with his grandmother," said Venetia. "She hath an affection for him, and sends for him often."

But will not receive you, Bristol thought; Mary Digby was inflexible. He told himself that he resolved to improve the position of Kenelm's wife; she lived prudently now, and it was time the past was forgotten. Bristol warmed his hands at the fire, and began to tell Venetia the contents of Kenelm's letter. She listened patiently, but it was evident she did not understand the workings of ships. By the time he finished, tears stood in the hazel eyes, and Venetia said: "He did not write to me, after the first. I fear he hath forgot me."

"Never that. You are the love of his life. He needs to prove himself, and afterwards will return to you with joy; believe me, I know him." He was full of sorrow while he knew you were unfaithful, that was all, he thought: but did not say it aloud.

"I hope that it is true," she said. "I live for his return, whenever that may be. He hath been gone now many months, and knows not his youngest by sight. Will you see the child?"

He assented, and presently the nurse brought down a cheerful bundle of warm clothes, set him down and they watched while John Digby crawled about the floor. He had features both of his father and of his mother. Venetia stared at him and did not attempt to touch or kiss him. Bristol said something to the purpose about the little fellow, patted him and gave him a wooden toy he had brought. The child stared solemnly, then began to shake it, giving it all his attention. "You may go now," said Venetia to the nurse, and John was taken away.

Afterwards Bristol said to her: "You have many callers here?" He knew the answer; there were few, except for Jonson, son of a bricklayer. He watched the rain start to fall in the street. "Continue as you are doing," he told her. "When your lord returns, it will gladden his heart that none may say a word against your discretion, that you have become a Lucretia." He smiled, and took her hands. "Kenelm's kin shall visit you, as I have done," he promised, "and I will come again."

"I would as soon the old lady did not. I am afraid of her."

"Poor Mary Digby hath had a bitter life. She loved her husband so greatly that when he was taken from her, nothing held any worth."

"She had her children."

"As you have. I pray God they may continue well, and yourself, Venetia."

He left her then, promising again to return, which he would do from time to time. In the end, he persuaded Kenelm's sisters to call, and of course Johnny, now

255

an officer of the King. The rest of the world would wait before acknowledging Kenelm Digby's wife, at least till his return; Bristol hoped that that would be soon, for the letter had not given tidings of any great fortune, rather the reverse.

In fact, Kenelm was seated in the company of the Bassa and other Algerian rulers in a square white house by the shore, drinking tea. The shadows were dark but in his mind they seemed full of colour; in his mind, also, above the talk about him, the memory of an odd thing he had seen lately in the town; a woman who had two thumbs on her left hand, and two of her daughters had it also, and a grandchild, but not her son. How could such a thing be? Yet he had seen it, therefore it was true. He brought himself back to what the Bassa was saying, in Italian; it appeared that he—they called him Hassan here— had been born in Venice. He was old now, and the wrinkles about his dark eyes gleamed a little as if with oil. He used his hands expressively to talk; they were lean and beautiful, the hands of a horseman. Presently he and Kenelm would ride out, to see a marvel he had been promised, a salt lake in the inland mountains. But meantime they spoke of England and her relations, if such they were, with the tough walnut-skinned men who had permitted Digby's ships to lie five weeks in the bay, if only because Hassan had taken a liking to his company. Otherwise they would have been fired or taken, and the crew seized as slaves. Kenelm hoped, by using his tongue persuasively, to buy the freedom of those other Christians who had been long held in slavery here. One, a man older than Hassan, passed about presently refilling the tea-cups. The beverage was scented and sweet; Kenelm had developed a liking for it, as there was no wine drunk in this company.

"Your English have not treated my people kindly," said Hassan, no doubt to placate the Duana, who was present in his turban and who evidently resented his chief's liking for the newcome Christian seafarer. His face was impassive, almost hidden in the folds of his robes except for the eyes, and he did not drink.

Kenelm made himself answer as he had done already many times. "Illustrious, my master the King of England said to me before I sailed that he had a great desire to be as a brother to you, and wished me to exercise all my wits to that end." He had, God knew, done so frequently; but they talked in circles.

"I tell you, more than a month before your coming here we had your Consul out of his house to be burned; and it may yet happen."

Digby tried to save Friswell, thinking that if the latter would develop the gift of laughter he might not be so easily for the burning; but the Consul remained a worthy man, stiff and grave. He was not present.

"You know well," said the Duana slowly in difficult French, "that the Frenchmen treated with us and would destroy you English in the straits, if they can. I say it is not for us to aid the enemies of our friends."

"But my master would be your friend also, and he is married to a French king's daughter." There had been nothing, beyond the movements of a heavy leather curtain embroidered with beads, to indicate that women mattered in the lives of

Hassan and his fellows; but they were there beyond the curtain, and had brewed the tea. The Duana's enigmatic face relaxed, and he gave a nod, as if he were satisfied.

"We should not make enemies for ourselves, it is granted," Hassan said. "We are at present fighting to throw off the yoke of the Turk, who was too long our master." A peculiar expression of loathing crossed his face, and Kenelm made up his mind that, on their next ride together, he would try to find out more about that hatred, and its cause. He was fascinated by this new world he had found, with its different values, its alien colours, the dark silent men seated in indigo robes like some part of the very shadows they sought. Yet old Hassan Bassa was a friend; he returned his thoughts to him. "The Turk is busied against Persia at present, is it not so?" he asked. "He will have little leisure to make further war in your time, or in your sons' time. Let us make our own peace."

In the end, he achieved it, but not in writing; they promised no more harassment of English merchants in the ports following losses of their own at sea, but instead vowed they would inform King Charles. Kenelm took leave to doubt the likelihood, but he wanted to get his fleet off, and the Christian slaves released, and must give something in exchange. By the end he gave thirty-three pounds per head for two score slaves, at any age; this being, evidently, the cost of their maintenance. And the sails of English ships would no longer be seized by Algerians in the harbour. He also, somehow, arranged for Friswell to be repaid a debt they owed him; as for his burning, that was postponed on the promise of continuing justice from the King of England.

Kenelm rode out with Hassan Bassa presently; it was towards evening and the day had begun to cool. The high-bred horses were so beautiful, with their muscles rippling beneath their satiny coats, that Kenelm would have liked to offer to purchase some, but there was no saying what they would suffer on the voyage and he doubted if the owners would let them go. But what fine progeny would result from breeding these Arabs with English mares! It was a dream, and would remain one; but Kenelm remembered it often, when the good smell of horse-sweat in the hot sun would return to him, with the musty aroma of the saddle-cloths and the dry gleam of the reins of scarlet leather, and the flying manes loosened with their speed, making him enjoy the race with the old Bassa, who was a superb rider but no better than Everard Digby's son. When they paused in the shade of a jagged rock Kenelm began to speak of his father, and of how he had taken joy in hunting from dawn till dusk, long ago. These horses would have delighted his heart; Kenelm remembered hearing that six thousand of them had galloped to the taking of Tunis: what a sight that must have been!

"And you?" said Hassan; his eyes crinkling against the blowing sand; a light wind had come up, cooling the horses. "I spear the wild boar with some pleasure," said Kenelm. It was true, he had had some hunting here, and even in Portugal on the way. "But it is a greater pleasure to talk with a wise man," he said suddenly. "Tell me of yourself, illustrious, if you will."

The other turned his head and Kenelm saw his eyes, their whites yellowed a little with age, regard him like some wary animal. "I am as you see me," the Bassa said. "The Algerians are robbers and I am their leader. What more would you know?"

"All you have to tell. I delight in meeting men of knowledge, no matter of what sort. I am forever after some new thing." He thought of his laboratory at home, the flasks and alembics grown dusty and cold till his return; and of Galileo and his talk of the earth and the sun. Yet when Hassan answered he found himself listening with pity and attention only for that of which the older man spoke, while the shadows jutted below the rock and the salt lake lay blue and glazed in the evening sun.

"I? I was a galley-slave with the Turks at Lepanto."

He dismounted, handing the reins to a Tuareg boy who had ridden behind them, his headdress veiling his face wholly after the manner of his tribe. Kenelm did likewise, and the two men walked together about the steep lake shore, seeing the idle lake but remembering, envisaging, another sea, with galleys and warships rocking upon it, and Don John of Austria with his yellow curled hair making war against the infidel with men of courage from every land in the West.

"I was a Venetian," said Hassan. "When I was a boy I went to sea; we were poor, and I wanted to come home to my mother a rich man. But the Turk took our ship before she was well out of the Adriatic, and the next fifteen years I spent on a galley bench, toiling and sitting in my own excrement like the rest. Later they made me overseer, and I whipped others as I had been whipped; no matter. Afterwards I saved enough to buy a share in my own boat, then a ship of my own. But that was later. I can remember Lepanto, and how the captured *Capitana* galley had a stuffed dried Christian commander's skin nailed to its prow. He had been one of the defenders of Famagusta. They beheaded the other three, but Bragadino was the bravest. They flayed him alive publicly, then took the skin and did with it as I have said. I believe the sight heartened the Christians so as to make them win the day. By then, I was neither Christian nor Turk, only lived from day to day as I might.

Name of God! I took my turn. It was I who burned, at last, the great wooden image of John the Baptist that had been seized long since from the Knights of Malta, and I who hung up their white-crossed shields above the arched gate at Marina. I was a ruler by then. I cannot say, therefore, that your English will think of me as a friend."

"The old Faith is gone in England now, that men fought for, and for which my father died. They do not have images now, except in secret." He remembered with regret that he had lately paid his own faith little heed, although he had always knelt at his prayers as the *Eagle* sailed south. He stretched out a hand and the Barbary pirate took it. "We are friends," said Kenelm, "and I will pray for you."

Despite all this friendship Kenelm discovered that some of the men in Stradling's ship had tried to waylay an Algerian vessel. He put the ringleader in chains, lectured the rest, and replenished his crew with redeemed captives. By the end of the month he weighed anchor, making for Majorca, in search of fresh fruit; also, though he kept it to himself, a further prize ship of a large size, if he might, and richly laden.

He took his prize at last, including the sattia he craved, but the first ship was one he had notice of after a raid by his men ashore, one early evening. There had been a fishing-boat there whose crew jerked awake and leaped overboard, thinking the swarming Englishmen with their sunburnt skins to be Turks. One man they took, and he gave them notice of some ships in the bay, but these all had watchtowers and brass cannon, yet Kenelm, nothing loath, gave the order to attack. They took a frigate with much wine aboard; that was the beginning of it, and the sattia, which rode at anchor, he took also and leaped aboard her.

She drew only a small draught, and Kenelm made sail to where the rest lay at anchor, despite shots from the brass cannon of the nearer ships, which peppered the water in a now familiar pattern. The sattia was taken under much fire, with two of his men killed and a half-dozen wounded, among them some of his new men from Algiers, who were good carpenters. The guns and muskets kept on firing as he sailed off, the great prize behind him, towing meekly.

Then there was a storm. In all of his voyaging he had never encountered one so fierce, and first of all he lost a boat and its crew, then the prize itself, which sank behind the high waves and they could not save her: they barely saved themselves. Kenelm almost wept; she had been very rich, and the booty he had not yet had time to see was gone down; well, it was his fate.

"Where are we?" he called, and was told the place, full of jagged ugly rocks, was off the coast of Sicily. They were in acute danger, and dropped anchor till the angry storm had passed; suddenly, as is the way in such places, there was nothing to be seen but the calm sea. What a mistress she was, sometimes furious, sometimes calm and sweet! But he would always regret the lost prize; nothing more was seen or heard of her.

He had only one ship left; formerly there had been seven, and the riches from the sattia would have paid all the expenses of the voyage. But at least he was not now undermanned; he walked among the men, tending their wounds and talking to those who had just come aboard at Tunis and still spoke English hesitantly, as if it had become a foreign tongue. They rounded Cape Passaro, then made north for the Straits of Messina. On the way he took another prize, whose captain had stood out against him with shouting and then shot. "We stood at her, and she at us boldly," he wrote later. After some acrimony a shot of theirs broke off the other ship's topsails, and he would have fought further, but the men refused; they were weary of fighting, and the strange ship followed them now peacefully. She had many guns and had corn in her hold; it was better than nothing, after all. But she was leaky, and Kenelm decided to sail to the Greek islands to sell the corn. There was no news of the rest of the fleet; and next day was Easter.

To his joy, afterwards on the emerald sea he saw the rest of his little fleet, Stradling's ship and the rest, advancing towards them, though not the prizes. He welcomed Stradling on board with great pleasure, and found the latter red-faced and a trifle drunk; they had been able to take some wine on board and had drunk too much of it. "We almost caught this, and that," Sir Edward was explaining, but Kenelm burst out laughing. "You could not see so far, my friend," he assured the Vice-Admiral. "We will head for Zante."

They hailed two English ships on the way, and heard news that their prizes were after all safe, but that corn had already been sold that day on the harbour at Zante. They made, accordingly, for Cephalonia instead; rejoicing in the golden air and the dark, eternally blue sea, with its islands encrusted with emerald and gold, each one different from the last, rising out of the veils of the dawn. Already he had made up his mind to explore, select, return, take his time and write of it all, but only after some noble deed should be done. What this must be first came to him on passing by Cyprus and seeing the city of Famagusta which the flayed Bragadino had defended so bravely long ago. What perfidy to punish him in such a way! Anger rose in Kenelm, and a kind of memory, as if he himself had been present in those times, with that cruelty. He would sail against the Turk as he might, on this latter day.

He swept at last into the Bay of Iskanderun, where Syria joined Asia Minor. The men called it Scanderoon. He had lately had trouble with them, having to put some in chains and deploy others to the rest of the ships, so that they could no longer plot against him; they wanted their money from the prizes, and were sullen. But now every man was alert, awaiting four Frenchmen said to be lying in Scanderoon harbour, with aboard, a hundred thousand reals of eight. It was a fortune, worth pursuing; even King Charles's French Queen might be pleased if they brought such a sum home.

But there were Venetian ships guarding the prize. What he did not know until he sailed towards them was that some of these were like floating castles, great galleasses castellated fore and aft, their three lateen-rigged masts supported by thirty-two banks of double oars, a half-dozen slaves to each. Kenelm took counsel with himself, while the light wind blew in his long beard and shaggy pirate's hair; he cast his mind back to stories he had heard of the Armada once sent against England. Had not the little English ships made fools of King Philip's proud galleons then? He would do the same now, moving swiftly by reason of small size. He heard eight rounds thunder out, then began to fire on the Venetians. This was not a salute, he knew, but war.

He coasted in below the galleasses' bulk at last, maiming their oars by virtue of their unwieldy size and his mobility. He ordered his little ships to swerve about with the favourable wind in the great sweep of the harbour. They put out irons to grapple, as had been done since the time of the Caesars. Then Kenelm let his men board the Venetians and fight. The thunder and smoke of cannon, the screams of drawn blood and reek of shot and hacked flesh, came; he himself was not wounded, any more than he had been in France and Spain. At the back of his mind floated the remembrance that he had sent polite letters to the Venetians and the English in the bay, but what did that signify now?

There had been no reply; well, let them see to it. Beyond, in the clear air, the four gold-laden French ships waited. After the fight Kenelm pursued them without let, and took them at last with a fierce joy in the victory. But when he and his men rushed down into the dark yawning holds they were empty; not a single gold coin on any captured ship. It had been taken ashore safely from the first two, the third and the fourth. There would be no treasure for the King.

Kenelm acknowledged his disappointment, hearing the chatter of French disturb the warm air, then cease with assurance. He had taken three of the ships and let the fourth run aground; so much he would at least bring home with him. Sweating beneath his half-armour at last—it had been a June day—he called the men back. Havoc had done its worst in the peaceful bay; many were wounded and dead, though Kenelm was certain he had lost only two men. There were enough left to withdraw along the coast, whence the authorities were anxious, by now, to be rid of him. If he had known of it, many English, including the Vice-Consul, were thrown into prison in Aleppo because of the battle and had to be rescued, but not by Kenelm, later with a ransom of much gold. The last thing he remembered, in fact, before putting out to sea was the figure of a consular officer on shore, hat awry, waving at him urgently to depart.

On the Grecian isle he chose he was able to remember it all. Some of the men had sailed on to Delos of the archaic stone lions; leaving the captain time to reflect. It was pleasant here; perhaps for the first time in his life there was no haste about anything. The sky was the colour of purple grapes in the strange clear light that showed the island pale gold, with its ruined stones lying about like giant marbles. Kenelm examined the interesting rubble, full of the glory that had been Greece before the Turks came. He began to collect objects to take with him home, though one beautiful frieze of four carven figures was too heavy to move even with all hands.

But Kenelm selected an inscribed Doric plinth for the King, some statues and other marble bases, golden with the sun, perfectly and symmetrically formed. Then he sat down to write. The urgency of this was first made known to him when the island's Turks pressed their hospitality, and not only gave him partridges and wine, but would have given him their women as well. The olive complexions were smooth and beautiful, the breasts and writhing hips fine; but he would not betray Venetia. In other words, he was by himself to do as he chose. He chose to write everything that came into his head, while the olives ripened and the fishermen cast out their evening nets to sea. His ship waited; everything waited; when he chose, but not before, he would return to England.

The months passed, and he became ever more diverted with his own company, the profusion of ideas, the flowing of the sepia ink on paper; his writings, the returning cult of Venetia. By now it seemed to him that all his toil had been for her, his trophies gained to lay with honour at her feet. But about then news filtered through to that remoteness of an unexpected kind; and Kenelm wanted at once to be at home. On the point of setting out for a renewed campaign against France, to redeem his own lost honour over the Île de Rhé, Buckingham had been stabbed to death by a discontented subaltern named John Felton.

Kenelm set sail, certain now that his fortunes were mended, and, not without further adventures, journeyed home.

King Charles had been deep in mourning for his friend Buckingham, but he made himself forget the death for the time, and arranged a joyous homecoming for Kenelm Digby. There would be difficulties with the foreign authorities who had suffered from the fight, particularly the Venetians, and it had all been for nothing when coolly looked at: but England's honour, of which she was always sensible and which, between the French war and the Spanish refusals, had been somewhat tarnished, was now redeemed, and the hero of the hour was coming home. The King turned to his Queen, for the pair had grown close since Buckingham's death and by now nothing would interrupt their care for one another. The little French princess who had come to England at first had been a child, and in ways always would be so, for

Henrietta Maria had a quick temper and a stubborn mind; but she was very pretty, with delicately curling dark hair and bright eyes, and her choice of clothes was exquisite; also, she loved her husband.

Kenelm rode to Court after his warm greeting at Woolwich by Lord Bristol, now freed of his great enemy. The Grecian plinth and other objects Kenelm had brought back were set out and admired, and at Whitehall courtiers thronged to meet him, to congratulate him, to ask him to dinner. He would reap rewards that sounded grander than they were, for by the end, with taxes, they would bring in little money; Commissioner of the King's Navy, for a man who had made his first voyage in command at sea; Commissioner to Virginia, the new colony which might or might not bring a fortune in tobacco; a member of New England's Council, though most who went out there were Dissenters and Kenelm was still a Papist; a fee-farm at Bradley Manor; profits from sealing-wax patents in Wales; trading rights of three separate regions of the Gold Coast in West Africa.

There was even a thirty-year monopoly

in Canadian furs and beaver, much used for hats. A suggestion that Kenelm should be made a Fellow of St. John's, Cambridge, was however refused; Cambridge was a Puritan stronghold.

Kenelm saw the King more than once about his own new duties as a naval officer working with the Admiralty (which body was much disturbed). "My father built few ships," Charles said to him, his mournful dark eyes fixed on Kenelm's sunburnt face, as if in envy of his prodigious energies. Kenelm knew of the bad state of the King's navy; it was a byword and half the vessels could never put to sea. "Our island, sire, should master the oceans; after all we are surrounded by them," he said. "If Your Majesty wills it, I can order estimates for building new ships. Wars now are fought at sea; we should be ready."

"It will cost money," said the King, "and that is not plentiful." His face was rueful, and Kenelm guessed that the extravagances of James's reign had left little in the royal coffers, and Charles himself had to beg Parliament for every penny, which was given grudgingly if at all. "I will serve you as well as my poor powers afford," Kenelm promised, and several times rode down to Deptford to study, inspect and prepare. Britain's navy should be a matter for pride, not shame, when he was done, he promised himself. Meantime he returned home, to Venetia.

She had welcomed him with open arms. The new child, John, was toddling; young Kenelm had grown into a handsome boy of four, a trifle shy at first, but soon laughing and playing with his father, sitting on his great broad knee and listening to his tales of the islands where fruit could be plucked from the trees and the sun shone always. It was a peaceful and happy time; Kenelm was especially pleased that Venetia had conducted herself with blameless prudence during his absence; there was not a whisper now against her. She was as beautiful as ever, and after his merry homecoming soon pregnant again; in all he was to give her a child a year for the whole of their marriage, except for the two years he had been away.

He loved to go home, but meantime the Admiralty work absorbed him, or perhaps less the work itself than the personages he met. Travellers came to Trinity House, telling of their strange experiences at sea; there was talk of sextants, stars, and Galileo. If the earth moved round the sun, not otherwise as had formerly been taught, could it not be that other accepted values were likewise valueless? It was necessary to experiment; without experiment there could be no knowledge. He drank in the heady talk, listening, contributing. Howell, whose hand he had cured with the Powder of Sympathy some years before, came often, his beard now almost white. "I saw," Kenelm remembered his saying, "such prodigious things daily done these few years that I had resolved with myself to give over wondering at anything."

But Digby still wondered at everything. He would never lose this wonder at all the world, the way things changed; yet stayed the same; why was one crested newt coloured brightly, the other plain? Was it true that an island near where he had stayed in the Mediterranean lately had devils on it, not men, and the devils would come out by night with the light of a lamp they lit, to loosen the cables of the ships lying there? Was it true that animals could be formed out of sticks? Always it was something that someone else had said, which would have to be proven by oneself. Kenelm assembled sticks in his laboratory and put them to various tests; none made an animal, but could the reason not be that he had not found the correct treatment?

Was Howell right in saying that a man in pied clothing in Germany had piped and led all the children of a town away through an opening in a hill so that they never returned? Howell said he believed it was true. But did that mean it was so? yet there were nearer wonders to be investigated here in England. He set about it in his enthusiastic way. Venetia, growing in pregnancy, sat with the children and was glad when he would amble in, his head full of science, his hair tousled where he had run his hands through it, writing, thinking. It was beginning to grow thin over the forehead, the curly hair; the suns of Greece had scorched it. "Can it be true," Kenelm would say, "that a toad can develop from a duck? They say it can happen." And he would dream away, thinking how to prove it, and quacking ducks would be brought to the laboratory, but nothing could be proved except that sometimes they laid eggs which contained not toads, but ducklings.

Meantime the wooden skeletons of the King's new ships rose against the sky at Deptford, and the new Commissioner for the Navy would stride about as he had once done on the deck of the *Eagle*, making suggestions, measuring, talking with the men as they worked with their hammers and saws. And the King began to think of a new way of raising money to build more ships, and soon a landowner named Hampden would be sent to prison, for refusing to pay the suggested tax. Digby himself was now rich and then again poor, for the recusancy fines were still in force despite the Queen's Papistry; Kenelm paid them absently, for he still had little time to devote to religion.

"You have struck your blow in the world; now it is time to think of your soul. I had the moulding of it at Oxford; surely I know you as well as any man."

Kenelm smiled to himself; Laud, Bishop of London, his quick precise gestures causing his lawn sleeves to vibrate with the fluttering motion of moth's wings, deceived himself. It was Tom Allen, if any, who had moulded Kenelm. Yet the gentle precise words of the King's rising prelate made Laud seem almost a saint, and it was difficult to credit the fact that the great churchman had lately allowed the branding and mutilation of a dissenting minister who had published a broadside against all bishops. Laud's small stature was made smaller still beside the huge form of Kenelm Digby.

"The King desires the spiritual union of all his people," said the Bishop, "if the Pope would but meet him halfway. But how can a foreign potentate understand the spirit of England? Our church is founded, uniquely, on that spirit; we have the continuity of succession, the reverence, the occasions." He said nothing of the Body of Christ, and Kenelm himself shied away from the ultimate argument. Was the Faith for which his father had died any more, nowadays, than a weak memory, shored up by a few brave men who came from abroad and conducted their untiring mission in danger of their lives, among the poor? He knew of that; yet, here at Court, it did not touch him as greatly as the sight of places given to others, and himself left out.

"By law, you should be imprisoned; you know it," said Laud in too clear a voice. It was true; despite the Queen's religion and her secret help for Catholics, they had little other. The old Faith had become a furtive hunted thing, without promise. He thought of it, and of the last time he had assisted at Mass secretly, in a house in Dorset.

"In Spain I did not like them, it is true. But here—" He thought of the patient Catholic families paying fine after fine for recusancy, as his mother still did; and had not the Pope fettered Galileo himself for his discoveries until their worth was proved? He thought of his own visit to St. Peter's, long ago; had it meant anything to him other than a visit to an Italian prince? He knew within himself that it had; and thrust down the memory of the Fisherman's Ring.

"Rome fetters reason," said Bishop Laud predictably. It mattered what a man was to himself; there was this new dissension, Quakerism, where men kept on their hats and would not swear in court. The Bishop almost crossed himself, then recalled that he had lately been offered a cardinal's hat twice over and had declined both offers. The Church of England was unique, personal, productive of worldly gain.

Kenelm was to think it over for a year, surrounded by his scrambling and increasing children: by now there were four, and a fifth on the way. He had begun to thirst for worldly recognition following his notable voyage to Scanderoon. His enemies were cast down; even Queen Marie de Médicis was cast from her place in France and in poverty, soon to batten on the charity of her son-in-law the King of England. One must move with the times: he owed it to his sons to ensure that a place in the world was theirs. He caressed young Kenelm, growing into a splendid boy; and at last took the Anglican sacrament at Whitehall, to the satisfaction of observers.

The King's deep knowledge of painting led him to invite Peter Paul Rubens, the

Fleming noted for his flesh-tones on canvas, to design a ceiling for the Banqueting House in Whitehall. For a long time scaffolding concealed the coming marvel, which proved at last to be an apotheosis of King James, portraying that monarch with his grey hairs looking up expectantly into Heaven, surrounded by appropriate angelic forces. With the Queen's altarpiece, Rubens would accordingly be known in England for more than his rumoured *affaire* with Marie de Médicis, in trouble as usual and said to be so poor she had to burn her furniture to light a fire.

Kenelm and Venetia inspected the new ceiling together, she in a becoming beaver hat with a wide brim and a plume; he was proud of her beauty, to which he felt Rubens himself would not do justice; in Kenelm's opinion the painter was too coarse, his female nudes overweighted. But soon Rubens' pupil, Anthony Van Dyck, whom Kenelm had already met in Rome, came to England at the King's wish. He painted Charles and Henrietta Maria not as they were, but as they should be; the exquisite frailty of his satin and lace set off his undoubted handling of human expression. Under his hands the little Queen blossomed into beauty, with a crown set back on her hair or a flame-coloured bow on the dove-grey satin dress she wore. Charles himself, short-legged and shy, was transformed into a godlike being astride a great-horse, or in wide hat and scarlet breeches holding his mount's bridle. The Court flocked to be portrayed, regardless of van Dyck's sensational fees. Kenelm, of course, wanted the painter to paint Venetia and their growing family as well as himself.

They arrived at the Blackfriars studio as other eminent company was leaving; the Earl and Countess of Arundel. The Earl, who had been brought up strictly by his mother and whose father had died under attainder in the Tower, owed his wife his fortune; Countess Aletheia was a Talbot, Bess of Hardwick's granddaughter, and she inherited immense wealth and many coalfields. Arundel himself, like his wife, had travelled abroad, and was so knowl-edgeable about art and antiquities that the King often consulted him before purchase.

Arundel and Kenelm had met

frequently at Court; the Earl's bearded face somewhat resembled the King's with its dark eyes and lean features; he wore a long gown, which made him seem older than he was. Lady Arundel was tall, stout, and majestic, except that she had features like a mouse. The pair greeted Kenelm, and Venetia sank in the correct depth of curtsey from a knight's wife to an earl's. Lady Arundel made a slight, frigid acknowledgement; one could never be sure about Digby's Venetia. But Kenelm pressed his wife's arm as they ascended to the light, bright studio with its windows looking out on to the Thames, where the elegant Fleming who had become the Court's most fashionable portrait-painter worked amid luxury he could now well afford. Van Dyck came forward eagerly, his brushes still in his hand.

"Digby! Digby! This is a delight. We will find the Philosopher's Stone together, perhaps?"

He poured wine for them. The double Arundel portrait, almost completed, stood on its easel, my lady resplendent in a coronet and holding an astrolabe in her hands, its burnished metal shining gold.

"I want you," said Kenelm, "to paint my wife as Prudence."

Venetia opened her eyes wide in the way she had. Van Dyck bowed to hide his smile. Lady Digby was certainly a most beautiful woman and he could make her seem even more so, but from all he had heard—

"You will paint her holding down the serpent of Rumour and caressing a dove of Peace. When do the sittings begin?"

The half-finished portrait was much admired and its allegory noted. Venetia's exquisite hair, eyes and skin were shown in all their brightness, and her slender, beautiful hands disposed as Kenelm had ordered; the serpent duly quenched in one, while the other stroked a soft white dove. Everyone came to view it, and perhaps the Court grew kinder to Venetia than it had been; but she troubled it little nowadays, she had no leisure.

Van Dyck and Kenelm withdrew to their chemical experiments in course, but later there would be more portraits, of Privy Councillor Digby, his wife and growing family; by the end three sons alive and one daughter, for a child died. But the last portrait of all would be of Digby himself in mourning, his small hands helplessly spread out against his cloak.

Digby began, despite his desertion of the Catholic Church, to see much about Court of the Queen, whom he admired as a woman, not strictly a beauty; but her love for her husband was by now admirable, and van Dyck and others had painted her oval face and small figure, attired in exquisite clothes, with a crown set becomingly at the back of her curled dark head and, lately, her children about her. Kenelm had first come upon the Prince of Wales as a large baby in a lace cap, dark as a Moor, grasping his coral rattle. By now there were others, and it was known the King enjoyed the company of his children as well as that of his wife. There was a pretty princess named Mary and a new, fair-haired baby, James.

Kenelm, with his own family increasing, regarded the young Princess with wistfulness; he had no feeling for his own small daughter, but took pride in his sons. Today he was to embark on a new adventure, or rather one he had tried already, abroad; he was to go to a séance. He knew well enough that the Catholic Church frowned on these, for he had attended one abroad, and part of the thrilling experience of forbidden fruit tempted him again; also, he was curious to see if there could be any result on this occasion and, if so, what; would his father's spirit come to him, as Samuel had to the witch of Endor? But when he joined hands at last with others at the table, there was no comfort, only meaningless words; and he strode out again presently into the bright day.

He had been thinking of the Queen, and it was in the nature of coincidence that a coach drew up by him, with outriders, in which she sat with her friend and familiar, Lady Carlisle. Digby did not like the latter; the Countess's painted face was too smooth, and she agreed with everybody. But he entered the coach, doffing his hat and kissing Henrietta Maria's small white hand. She patted the seat by her.

"I am glad to see you, Sir Kenelm," she said in her charmingly accented English, and smiled at him with closed rouged lips, for her teeth stuck out. "You are the very person to whom I would like to entrust an errand."

"Two errands," said Lucy Carlisle, who knew everything the Queen did. Kenelm felt a rush of dislike, no doubt, he reminded himself, without reason. He said to Henrietta Maria: "Your Majesty may safely trust me with her life, if need be."

The Queen laughed. "It is not that, or not yet," she said without awareness of prophecy. "I would like you, sir, to deliver two purses of money for me to two separate gentlemen, each of whom is worthy of it. You will find Mr. Morse at St. Giles's and Mr. Southworth at the hither end of Westminster, in the poor quarter. No one must follow you, you understand?" The dark eyes fixed themselves on him and he was aware of a certain opaque quality in the bright gaze. He promised secrecy, while wondering at the Queen's choice of a known renegade for a confidential errand. But perhaps for that reason he would be the last to be suspected and followed. He had known a kind of freedom since obeying Bishop Laud, a devil-may-care quality that reminded him of his own days of pirating, though without its discomforts.

He bowed his way out of the coach at Charing Cross, and made his way on foot to Westminster. As he passed by beggars cried out to him for silver and he flung some, being generous with his money and sorry for their state; but it was nothing to what he saw behind St. Margaret's, though there was no plague at this season.

Here lived Papists who might not qualify for poor-relief. The hovels—they could not be called houses—leaned towards one another so that no light was shed on the filthy street: men and women lay about in the shadows, unhoused, sick or hungry, their thin arms reaching out to him while others, in worse state, cared nothing whether he came or went. He saw children like skeletons, with great pot bellies full of wind, or perhaps worms; these showed in the excrement, which mingled with other offal in the gutter, and stank while almost itself alive with maggots. The place was crowded, as he imagined a charnel might be; he clutched the package the Queen had given him lest it be snatched away.

He hardly knew whom to ask concerning Mr. Southworth, but at mention of his name a thin scabbed man jerked his head towards the river, and Kenelm made his way through the rubble and the bodies of the living and half dead, and found a small-boned personage kneeling in the street, caring for a sick woman. His features were fine and he had a small light-brown beard. He wore, in defiance of the law, a priest's stole, and carried the Sacrament. The woman for whom he cared was dying and as she received the wafer on her tongue, those of her family who were nearby began to pray aloud and cross themselves. They were not the careful, sonorous Anglican prayers. Digby knelt down by the priest, much moved, and asked his name.

"I am John Southworth." He spoke as a man will who has no fear. The calm eyes looked into Kenelm's and for some reason the other felt tears rise in his own. What had he lost? Could he himself do as this priest did, venturing health, fortune, life itself for the cause of Christ? He knew that he could not. Had he not lately forsworn this very Faith?

"Her Majesty sends you this," he said lamely. The large purse contained two smaller, and John Southworth received one of these, smiling thankfully. "May God bless Her Majesty, and you, my son," he said. "It will help these poor people." He spared time to look about him, sitting back on his heels. "This is not the worst time," he said. "It is worse in summer, when the plague comes. Then the doors, if there are any, are shut and marked and few will collect the dead for fear of infection. Some food at least can be bought for these poor souls now, which may give them strength for the time."

"And you?" said Kenelm. The priest seemed untroubled. John Southworth laughed, showing teeth that were worn and brown; he was not a young man. "I?" he said. "I am these many years out of the Clink on parole. When it suits them, they will come for me again. Until then, I can do my work. My son, are you a Catholic that you come here to me? I do not know you."

Kenelm felt himself flushing. "No," he said briefly, but the other did not drop his gaze; indeed it seemed to soften. Kenelm would never forget the expression of deep pity on the fine face. No doubt the Queen had sent him, the renegade, here of purpose.

"I will pray for you," John Southworth said quietly. He looked at the second purse which lay within the larger. "That is for my fellow-priest at St. Giles, is it not?" he said. "If you will save yourself a journey, I should meet with him this evening; I say 'should' because none of us are certain, from one hour to the next, that we will be left free to meet."

Kenelm thrust the purse into his hand. "Ay, pray for me," he said thickly. His shame, and the stench of the poor people, followed him as he stumbled out and on to the open way again. He walked for long through the evening air, half sorry that he had not gone to meet Henry Morse at St. Giles's. John Southworth, he was certain, was a saint: all priests were saints; what other men would expose themselves to the risk of an appalling death for the sake of ministering to the poor souls of England? Laud would not. Or did he misjudge the strict, scholarly, steadily promoted Bishop of London? Perhaps Laud had merely not been tried in such ways: or not yet.

Kenelm slid out of bed carefully, so as not to wake Venetia, who had not been well. He adjusted the curtain carefully as he left, with the memory of her flushed cheek turned away from him, her head on her hand. He dressed quickly in old clothes, without calling his valet; then went to his laboratory, where he also prepared dishes daily. Today he would make snail broth to strengthen Venetia, in the same way as he always made unguents and tinctures for her complexion. He regarded the snails, which had come fresh yesterday from a pond near Gothurst, with approval; they had the right colour of house, a white and grey. He drained them from the pickle in which they had lain overnight, and began to pound them with parsley in a mortar. As he did so he was aware of being watched; his small daughter Margery stood at the door staring at him, still in her shift. He disliked Margery; she was sly. However he reproached himself, and because he so disliked the child tried to make amends. "Come and stir the broth," he said, "and then you shall carry it up to your mother."

But Margery said nothing, as was her way, and made off. Kenelm stirred the broth himself, still reflecting on his children. The best loved of all, little Everard, had died before he was three: and George was yet a baby. Of the rest, with Margery, he disliked young John, who seemed insolent: but loved Kenelm, who was growing into a fine strong boy, with courage and ready answers, yet modest with those. He smiled as he thought of young Kenelm; with his own new preferment at Court, the boy should have every chance when he was grown.

The broth was ready. He poured it into an earthenware bowl, and moving carefully carried it into the bedchamber. He set it on the bed-step that stood beside the poster, and drew the curtain open; Venetia still lay as he had left her, asleep. He called her name gently, then when she did not reply stretched out his hand to touch her cheek; the flush had gone and she was pale.

"Venetia."

She did not answer, and in a shock that

almost made his heart stop beating, he saw that she was dead.

His grief was terrible: at times he thought he would go mad. Somehow in the days that followed he had time to inform himself of other things than sorrow; there was scandal, it was said he had poisoned Venetia by feeding her capons fed with viper broth; indeed he had fed her the broth itself often, and she had felt the better for it. To poison her, who was the core and centre of his being? How could they even murmur of such a thing?

It was the King who consoled him. Charles ordered an autopsy, to clear Kenelm's name; this was done, and a huge gallstone found, also the brain by then was wasted away. But Kenelm had already sent for none other than van Dyck to paint Venetia as she lay dead; the painter laid a rose on her breast, and made the portrait with its petals falling; as with the flower, so with her body. The tears poured down Kenelm's face; he would hardly leave her, hardly see anyone. Once he was aware of young Kenelm's voice, and the boy's hand slipped into his. "You must come to see your mother," he heard himself tell the child, then: "Is she not beautiful?" He leaned over and rubbed at the cheeks a little, to bring the blood up; but it was sluggish with death: her lawn nightcap covered her brow.

It seemed as if Venetia would forever lie there in his mind, serenely lovely, an idol to be worshipped, an image before which to kneel; he did not admit to himself that this in part comforted him, as though he were free at last of the daily rub and grind of fortune, the things from which he had escaped once, to sail far away to Greece and write of his love there.

Young Kenelm stared, and said: "Yes, Father," and agreed that his mother was indeed beautiful, like a waxen saint grandmama kept hidden at Gothurst, neither breathing nor expected to; Mama had never been anything but a beautiful form to adore; she had not been like his nurse, who bustled about and ordered them all, or his tutors, to whom by now Kenelm was newly sent, and who ordered him also. Mama had been remote, unpossessed of either temper or fancy; she was someone for whom old Ben Jonson wrote poetry, and now was dead, and his father, whom Kenelm dearly loved, had tears pouring down his cheeks just like a child, like oneself.

Ben Jonson too was deep in grief, and would have liked to write celestial verses for this saddest of all sad occasions, but could think of nothing but worms; worms making holes in Venetia's ears in order that teardrops might hang in them like pendant jewels; worms writing the message of death itself on her white brow. He joined the many mourners who filled the house and overflowed into the garden, for Venetia had had many admirers for her charity as much as her beauty; among them was Dorset, who of late years had done no more than invite Kenelm and Venetia to dinner once a year, and then would only kiss Venetia's white hands.

When they shrouded her, they made a discovery, and brought it to Kenelm. He fingered its roughness absently; it was a hair shirt. Venetia had grown pious of late, perhaps while he himself was busied with his snails and vipers. It made no difference; he would always mourn her.

He left the children with their nurses and tutors and himself withdrew to Gresham College, nearby the Charterhouse. There he could think and, in a way, become a philosopher; he let his beard grow, and began to look as shaggy and unkempt as he had done at Algiers, but the eyes were sadder. He began to think of a memorial to Venetia, of lead overlaid with the finest copper; nothing should be spared in the setting up of it, her memory should stand forever in the modelling as much as in van Dyck's rendering of her in death. Kenelm paced his rooms planning it, and writing verses; he hardly saw a coach pass by, with an old woman inside in a black lawn cap. It was his old flame the Queen Dowager of France, Marie de Médicis, penniless and homeless, come to throw herself on the difficult charity of her English son-in-law, who already had troubles of his own. Kenelm was to meet her again; perhaps both he and she recalled the time at Angers when she had desired his body so passionately, long ago.

That was all in the past; the future was bleak also. The Great Fire which raged over London in the next generation, starting from a baker's shop, would destroy with so much else Venetia's tomb. The lead image, robbed of its copper, was seen by some passer-by in a shop, but soon melted down for the metal's value. She would be forgotten by all but a few.

Kenelm had taken a flower and burnt it to ashes, then tried to revive it again with a gentle and life-giving heat; but there was no life there. He experimented aimlessly with the weight of plants before and after burning; it came to him that there must be some substance out of the air which was necessary to them, but he could not isolate it. In the solitude of his laboratory he had made at Gresham he tried again, unsuccessfully, for the Philosopher's Stone.

It was like everything else in his life; sought after, longed for, slipping out of his grasp at the last moment, perhaps lost for ever. He began to feel a great dissatisfaction with himself over and above his grief; that last would be always with him. It was as though he were a ship without any rudder, his sails billowing and trimming to every wind. How could he cast anchor?

He knew that he would always be restless in mind and body. It was best to have some rock to founder on, if that were the term; a sure foundation beneath deep waters, which would not shift with the storms. He walked to and fro about his rooms in the college, then at last got his great mourning-cloak and tall Spanish hat, and went out. The wind was fresh and blew against him; he felt himself now a spar of wood, tossed about as if at sea. He moved without conscious direction, but found himself where he had wanted to be, for the time; Kemp's Yard behind Westminster.

"You must not commit yourself to returning to the Church because you are full of grief over your wife's death," said John Southworth. His eyes rested kindly on the huge distraught man in mourning who gesticulated with his hands as he talked, like a Frenchman. Kenelm spread them wider as he answered, despairingly. "I had not taken thought other than that the Church would be eager to receive me again," he said. The priest smiled.

"We do not force men against their better judgment," he said. "You say you left the Church because of worldly preferment."

"And conviction, a little, at the time. But I have thought of this for long, without perhaps knowing at first what it was I thought of. If you will not help me I am lost." He looked about him, at the poverty and pain; they made his own troubles seem small, even now.

"You are not lost if you have returned to God. Go home, my son, and think for another little space; then if you will, come again to me here. If I am gone do not search for me: as you will know, Father Morse was taken two or three years since, and died a martyr. I pray that it may come to me also, old as I am. They would not let me return to France, as I am much needed here; but, as I say, I may follow them when they least expect it." His eyes held deep certainty. What was this knowledge that came to good men? I am not one, thought Kenelm sadly.

"I will go to my mother at Gothurst for

a little," he said, and thrust silver into the priest's hand. "That is for hearing me, and for your poor."

"May God bless you," said John Southworth quietly. "I will pray that you find the right path. Remember me to your mother, and give her my blessing also."

Mary Digby had withered quietly over the years, and took little interest now in anything except her faith; she had shown no interest in the alterations Kenelm had made to Gothurst, the rendering of the place to look like a great ship and the garden displayed with its herbs and flowers growing in the shape of a gigantic anchor, kept in place by cement edges. Kenelm, she knew, always had his fancies, and nothing would do but that they must be given rein; as for herself, she would as soon be out of the world.

She had heard of Venetia's death with composure, and did her duty by her grandchildren as she might; they often came to stay with her, but were not here at present. Mary received Kenelm dressed in black, as he was himself; a string of silver rosary beads hung openly from her belt with her keys. It was less hard to be a practising Catholic than it had been, despite Father Morse's execution and the danger remaining to priests themselves, which even the Queen could not change.

Kenelm stumbled out with his story, but her expression did not alter. "It is time you looked to your soul," was all she told him. Were these not the very words Laud had used, years back? One could go back and forth, and never rest. He would rather have the certain rock, which had sustained his mother when her heart was dead within her. So it should be with him.

"Take me to a priest," he said, unable to wait. There might well be one in hiding here, in the secret place Nicholas Owen, Little John, had made long ago in his father's lifetime behind the upper third of the mullions. This was not so, but there was someone at the Vaux house. Kenelm visited him, confessed and was given absolution, heard Mass and received the Sacrament. Through all the rest of his life he would cleave to the Catholic Church, never weakening in that although there would be other weaknesses, common to all men.

His life was to be a puzzle to many, perhaps a cause of derision to some. He often read the letters his father Everard had written to him from prison, and more than once it occurred to him to ask himself if he had fulfilled all that had been hoped of him.

There is in none of these any thing wanting, that may be an impediment to truest Friendship, nor anything that may be added to them, but your own consent and particular desert each to other. Since then there is all cause in each of you for this love, do not deprive yourselves of that earthly happiness which God, Nature, and Time, offereth unto you . . .

Be that as it might, he was to achieve more things in more places than almost anyone of his generation, even though the achievement itself might be less than had been hoped.

He was to hear of Laud's execution, and

the King's: and, astonishingly, to become firm friends with Lord Protector Cromwell, each man seeing in the other some quality he had privately cherished. Digby, the widowed, exiled Chancellor to Queen Henrietta, went back and forth like a shuttle, in good times and in bad; in that same year of 1654 he watched on a day of storm and rain among the coaches, while the captured priest John Southworth, who had worked all his life for the poor, was dragged on a hurdle to Tyburn and, despite his age, hanged, drawn and quartered along with three counterfeit coiners. Neither ambassadors' pleas nor those of Kenelm himself had availed to save him. The judge had wept while passing sentence according to the law.

Kenelm resumed his travelling. He went from London to Paris, to Rome to hector the Pope for funds for the Queen; to Brussels, where he published a leaflet: to Holland, where he fought a duel. He had become a legend, if only because he was so strong he could lift a man sitting in a chair, using one arm only. He tried, unsuccessfully, to raise funds from the English Catholics in support of the new

King, Charles II: they were too hard-pressed to give him even promises. Kenelm was for a short time Privy Councillor, was imprisoned, freed, arrested again, sent to the Tower. He was set free, of course; but knew sorrow almost as great as that for the death of Venetia. His favourite son, Kenelm, was killed in the Civil War, and the second, John, he never dealt well with; the third, George, died, and he cared nothing for his daughter. By the end only Digby was left, a huge balding bearded old man of great charm and dinner-time wit, almost crippled with the stone, lecturing still on his Powder of Sympathy which he swore by; whether for this reason or not, he helped to found what was to become the Royal Society, elected a founder member. He died at last in one of a row of houses he had built for himself in Holborn, "the last fair house westward in the north portico of Covent Garden", and was mourned by his friends for a time, then forgotten as others are, while the world changed.

GUIDE
TO THE COLOUR CODING
OF
ULVERSCROFT BOOKS

Many of our readers have written to us expressing their appreciation for the way in which our colour coding has assisted them in selecting the Ulverscroft books of their choice. To remind everyone of our colour coding—this is as follows:

BLACK COVERS
Mysteries

★

BLUE COVERS
Romances

★

RED COVERS
Adventure Suspense and General Fiction

★

ORANGE COVERS
Westerns

★

GREEN COVERS
Non-Fiction

THE SHADOWS
OF THE CROWN TITLES
in the
Ulverscroft Large Print Series

ROMANCE TITLES
in the
Ulverscroft Large Print Series